MW01124623

I SHOULD HAVE WRITTEN A BOOK

A Sailor's Journey from Omaha Beach to Japan during World War II

Based on the World War II experiences of
William Grannetino

Written by his son,
Tom Grannetino

Suite 300 - 990 Fort St
Victoria, BC, V8V 3K2
Canada

www.friesenpress.com

First Edition — 2019

ISBN
978-1-5255-3596-3 (Hardcover)
978-1-5255-3597-0 (Paperback)
978-1-5255-3598-7 (eBook)

1. FICTION, HISTORICAL, WORLD WAR II

Distributed to the trade by The Ingram Book Company

[TABLE OF CONTENTS]

[PROLOGUE]

A LANDING CRAFT TANK (LCT) WAS an amphibious assault craft used during World War II to carry tanks, vehicles, or infantry from sea to shore. In many cases they were the first vehicles to reach the beaches, making them prime targets for enemy fire. They are best known for landings at the Normandy Beaches, in the Mediterranean, and on several Pacific islands.

[ODE TO THE LCT]

Here's to the men who sail the seas
on the bucking decks of the LCTs.
The battleships, cruisers and destroyers as well
get all the glory, the LCTs catch hell.

And when it's all over the work is all done
and the medals are given to the men who won,
and outfits are lauded by the power that be
forgotten as usual will be the LCT.

By Jim Howard, LCT (A) 2339 & LCT 244

Poems are made by fools like me, but only God can steer an LCT.
They have bestowed fond names on their vessels,
But the regular Navy's names for them are not so tender.
They call them Water Mules or Spitkits, Seagoing Jalopies,
Sea Jeep, or just plain Four Letter Words.

Author unknown

[ACKNOWLEDGMENT]

THANK YOU TO MY WIFE, Kathleen, for supporting me while I was writing and for supporting the idea of publishing this book. Also, a special thank you to author Carol Henn for all her guidance and help in getting this story from words on paper to a published book.

[DEDICATION]

THIS BOOK IS DEDICATED TO my grandchildren: Kyron Ahner, Megan Ahner Schmick, Stacy Ahner, Candis Keck, and Eric Keck. May all of you always remember your great-grandfather's service to our country and pass the spirit of these stories on to your children, grandchildren, and great-grandchildren.

[FOREWORD]

"I SHOULD HAVE WRITTEN A BOOK."

Those words have echoed through my mind more times than you can imagine. They are the words my dad repeated countless times as he told and retold me the stories of his World War II experiences.

Growing up, my brothers, sisters, and I heard stories of our father's time spent in the navy, be it the fact that he was at Omaha Beach on D-Day or the weeks spent at sea working as a crew member of a minesweeper off the coast of Japan at the end of the war. To tell you the truth, we did not know much more than that, and for the longest time they remained nothing more than stories of far-off places in a time long past.

Then came one Friday night back in 1998.

The movie *Saving Private Ryan* hit theaters in 1998, captivating audiences throughout the nation with its gruesome realism. The next time I saw my dad, I told him I had seen the movie and I asked him if he had seen it yet.

"Yes, I did," he replied, somewhat derisively.

"Was that what it was really like?"

"Yes ... and no. It was like that by the time the army got to the beach, but those Hollywood screenwriters certainly don't know the real history of the Omaha invasion. They didn't pay one bit of attention to what the navy and the 743rd Tank Battalions were doing immediately before the brave soldiers of the army's 29th Infantry Division started their assault."

That conversation sparked a four-hour exchange about Dad's landing on Omaha Beach and all of his World War II experiences. Everyone in my family knows that my dad had never been one to wear his feelings on his sleeve, but on that late Friday night, he exposed his bottled-up emotions by releasing a captivating recollection of his wartime experiences. As he recalled those D-Day stories in detail, he visibly shook with emotion as he brought new life to his memories by speaking them aloud. As he was telling the stories, he would rub his arms with both hands and stand up halfway out of his chair. Then, sitting back down, he would shake his head while he crossed his flexed arms and pulled his clenched fist close to his chest. Sometimes his voice would crack with emotion and he would stop talking, look away, and just stare at the floor for a few seconds or so. It's hard to imagine the fear he must have felt on D-Day, given that fifty-four years later he was shaking just telling the stories. I will never forget how emphatically he would say, "When we were on the beach, I *knew* I was going to die. I just kept wondering how long I would last." He told me this repeatedly.

Dad talked a great deal about two wartime associates. The first one was his commanding officer, Ensign Thomas Corker. He would always end his stories about Corker by saying, "That Corky was sure a nice fella', a real gentleman."

Then there was his good friend Tillins. I remember he would always laugh when talking about Tillins who, according to my dad's description, must have been the ship's funny man. Their friendship was forged while in the line of fire, as the two of them fought together on the battlefront on several occasions. Dad would always laugh after telling a "Tillins story," and he would end each one by telling me what Tillins' favorite line was, even during the most dire situations. Dad would proceed to do his Tillins impersonation, with a straight face and with his eyes extra wide open as he mimicked Tillins, saying, "You know, Bill, a fellow could get killed around here!"

It was with great pride that Dad described the Landing Craft Tank 9134(A), the amphibious landing craft he was assigned to during the D-Day invasion. When talking about D-Day, he would emphasize, "You know, those of us serving on the LCTs were the first Americans to hit the beach. We landed thirty minutes before the brave soldiers of the army's 29th Infantry Division."

When Dad talked about the opening scenes of *Saving Private Ryan* for the first time, he seemed to get a little angry and sharply said, "They're wrong about one thing for sure: In the movie when Tom Hanks reached the sea wall in the Dog Green sector on Omaha Beach, he was telling his radioman to inform command that no armor had made it ashore, that they had no DD tanks on Dog Green. That's 'bull' and not historically correct; the LCTs on the western end of Omaha had taken our tanks directly to the beach. We had the tanks there before Hanks' character would have been aboard a landing craft as it was making its final run toward the beaches."

Over the next ten years, Dad and I would talk about his World War II experiences almost every time we got together. When Dad was spending winters vacationing in Arizona, he would call every few weeks to say hello. We would begin with the formality of updating and discussing the current family news, but like iron to a magnet, our conversation would always return to talking for an hour or so about his wartime experiences.

Those conversations inspired me to make a trip to France in the late summer of 2006. Touring the beaches of Normandy with the help of a tour guide, I eventually found my way to the French commune of Vierville-sur-Mer, where I walked the Dog Green and Charlie sectors of Omaha Beach. It was when I got to the western end of the beach that the countless pictures my father's words had painted in my mind suddenly became real. I instantly recognize from my dad's descriptions the layout of the German gun emplacements and the terrain that had been described to me so many times. Staring out into the sea, I saw exactly where LCT 9134(A) had landed sixty-two years earlier. And in that moment, I realized I was literally walking in the footsteps of my father, and in my mind's eye, I was seeing everything my dad had experienced all those years ago.

Over the next five years that followed my 2006 trip to France, Dad developed Alzheimer's and lived out his final days in a nursing home before passing in 2011. His final two years in particular were spent suffering from the effects of the ruthless disease; he was sadly no longer able to remember my mother's name, the names of his kids, where he had lived, or most of what he had done over the course of his lifetime.

But somehow he never forgot the day he landed on Omaha Beach.

My weekly visits to the nursing home were spent conversing with my dad—to the best his condition would allow—about my current family affairs. Perhaps it was a need to share burdens long kept secret within him, or maybe it was just natural to communicate what he remembered clearly, but without fail our conversations would shift to his wartime experiences. To help him recall, I would start a statement about one of his experiences and he would enthusiastically take over and finish the thought I had started, as his voice filled with wonder, sorrow, and everything in between. He especially enjoyed talking about Corker and Tillins. Each time he recalled "Corky," he told me what a "nice fella'" he was and a "real gentleman." When remembering Tillins, he would do his impersonation as if it was the first time he had shown me. With a straight face and with his eyes open extra-wide, he would say as he had for the past twelve years, "You know, Bill, a fellow could get killed around here!"

For the sake of our family and especially my grandchildren, I decided to write down the stories of Dad's wartime experiences so they could be passed on to all his great-grandchildren and subsequent generations. I wrote this book as if I was my Father fulfilling that dream of finally writing down his war time experiences, hoping readers would better come to know the spirit of my Father. With that thought in mind, I included a few of the personal commentaries Dad shared with me as he was telling me his stories for the first time, that late Friday night in 1998.

Even though I had heard the stories many, many times over the next several years, when it came to writing them down, I realized I was missing a lot of information and didn't really have a full understanding of the actual succession of events and how they were connected to each other. Therefore, I pieced information together in the best fashion I could. While based in historical fact, and based on my father's firsthand wartime experiences, these stories are not intended to be completely accurate or precise in their detail. In many cases, I used my own imagination to create the stories that connected my dad's personal accounts. I also used my own thoughts and words as I put Dad's stories together in a logical sequence. My real motivation was to get into his mind and convey what he was feeling and thinking during the war. I tried to imbue his stories with his spirit and use his "voice," but when all is said and done, this book can be best described as a son's version of war stories based on his father's actual experiences during World War II.

It is my ultimate hope that you will come to understand who William Grannetino was and how his experiences in World War II played a large part in shaping his destiny.

Tom Grannetino

I SHOULD HAVE WRITTEN A BOOK

From the Recollections of Bill Grannetino

[CHAPTER 1]

Before I Landed

I WAS BORN WILLIAM JOHN GRANNETINO in Bath, Pennsylvania, in 1924 to the son of an Italian immigrant from Naples, Italy. His name was Andrew Grannetino, and my mother's name was Rose Cher Grannetino. She was from Hungary. The oldest of four children, I had two brothers and a sister. At the age of ten and in the middle of the Great Depression, I was burdened with responsibilities ordinarily only held by adults. My father and mother separated, after which time my father put me in charge of the family bills and the entire household's paperwork, as he was unable to read or write English. I also essentially raised my two brothers and my sister. Without a doubt, the changes that occurred in my family during the Great Depression ended my childhood and forced me to grow up very quickly.

Five years later and several inches taller, I got a job at the local filling station. For the next two-and-a-half years, I pumped gas and assisted the garage mechanic with automobile maintenance as well as complex tasks like rebuilding engines. While working there, I became a very competent mechanic. This work opportunity was financially beneficial for me and my family. Between my paycheck and my father's paycheck from his job working full-time in a cement mill, we had much more money than other families had during the Depression.

From Grade Ten to Grade Twelve I attended Broughal Trade School in Bethlehem, Pennsylvania. Another benefit of my early work experience was the acquisition of skills that enabled me to excel in my trade school studies, which in turn prepared me for a career as a mechanic. It felt good to be the only teenager in the neighborhood who had a dollar in his pocket. With the money that I consistently saved from my paycheck, I bought a brand new motorcycle from the Indian Motorcycle Manufacturing Company. I had a great time showing it off as I drove around town with the sun shining off the cherry red fuel tank and fenders, and the rough hum of the engine loudly bellowing my presence to those around the next street corner. So even during the Depression, life in the Grannetino household was, thankfully, pretty good compared to most other families.

During these years, everyone was aware of the trouble across the Atlantic. Germany and its Nazis had invaded Poland. Britain and France, in return, had declared war on Germany, and German troops had marched into Paris and occupied all of France. Next, Germany's Luftwaffe started bombing Britain. In retaliation, Britain fought back and began night bombing Berlin.

The world news was on everybody's mind, and it became a part of our everyday lives— to the point where every other conversation was about the war. I heard the older men who were regulars at the filling station talking about "this war in Europe." As I recall it, they all said the United States should "stay out of it" and that "this had nothing to do with us!" Several of these men had been in World War I, and perhaps the horrors they saw during those years still haunted them enough to discourage them from wanting to take action. It was their influence that caused me to be totally opposed to the idea of the United States getting involved in another war like the First World War. I had full respect for these veterans and trusted their opinions.

Then, on December 7, 1941, when I was seventeen years old and in my first half of the 12th grade, we heard the news that Pearl Harbor had been bombed by the Japanese. The phrase "actions speak louder than words" was never more true than on that day, because in that moment the minds of nearly every American were swayed, as the United States officially entered the war. Men just a little older than myself scrambled to enlist quickly, with the rate of enrollment going as fast as it took for them to sign their names on the dotted line. There was a sense of pride instilled in the hearts of America's young men, and Uncle Sam smiled kindly on those who were able-bodied and willing to risk their lives for Lady Liberty's honor.

Well, I don't really understand why, but I didn't feel moved enough as a patriot to enlist. Most likely it was all those years of influence by the World War I veterans at the filling station that caused me to be totally opposed to the idea of the United States getting involved in another war. If the Japanese started bombing the west coast of the United States, I would go to war in a minute. But to go fight somebody else's war overseas? Well, my opinion was "the hell with that." I didn't want to go to war, learn to march, shoot guns, or die overseas. I believed that the war was not my problem, and it seemed like there were plenty of other "gung-ho" young men who were seeking revenge by enlisting. I just hoped the war would be over before I got to draft age.

All around me the whole country was getting involved in the war effort. People started collecting scrap metal and rubber to help supply America's manufacturers with raw materials for supplying the war effort. Then the rationing of food and gas started as large quantities of both were funneled into the military. Next, everybody was buying bonds to finance the war while taxes went up. I wasn't really enthusiastic about all this.

In 1942, at the age of eighteen, I graduated high school. At that time the most recent war news was that the Japanese had lost the Battle of Midway, along with four aircraft carriers in the process. At home, we were all hoping that this meant the war in the Pacific was going to end soon. In Europe, the Germans were moving toward a fight in Russia and engaging the British in North Africa. Still, I was hopeful that somehow this war in Europe would come to an end before too long.

I had heard that the Chester, Pennsylvania, shipyards were paying big money and offering lots of overtime hours building ships for the war effort. More important than good wages, working in the shipyards would give me a draft deferment, meaning I wouldn't have to join the army because I was doing my service at home. Given the choice between building ships thousands of miles away from the war or exchanging bullets with Germans on the frontlines, I naturally chose the shipyards.

The minimum age for employees in the shipyards was eighteen. Within a few days after I graduated high school I was working for the Sun Ship Building and Dry Dock Company at their Chester, Pennsylvania, shipyards.

I rented a room nearby and went to work as a welder. I spent the next several months working long hours and earning good money, while any worries of being drafted faded from my mind. On Sundays I would return home to spend time with friends and family.

After about six months in the shipyards I became working partners with an older fellow named Wassel. We made more piece-rate money than any other welders in our crew because we both worked "smart." We became very familiar with the welding operations and learned how to sequence our work for the greatest efficiency. Wassel followed my lead, and before long we were equally productive. He didn't mind taking direction from a younger man, and I was thankful for that. Under my direction, Wassel and I saved lots of time by setting up smart, which gave us more welding time. We always worked shrewdly and maximized our production through the many good methods we had learned. Wassel and I became the most successful team on our crew. We were doing so well that our supervisor came to us one day and complimented us. Then he told Wassel that he was "doing such a good job" at training me, a younger man, that he had decided to give Wassel a raise and put him in charge of more men—in fact, the whole crew! After the supervisor was far enough away to hear us talk, Wassel looked at me and asked, "Now what am I to do?" I told Wassel not to worry, that I would work with him supervising these other guys. Over the next several months, things went well for Wassel, our whole crew and me. There was lots of work to be done and plenty of money to be made.

After working in the shipyards for almost a year, I returned home one weekend to find a letter sitting on the kitchen table. Emblazoned on the front of the envelope was the Seal of the United States government. I slowly peeled the envelope open to reveal its contents. Inside was the dreaded letter stating that I had been drafted. The war deferments regarding working in the shipyards had changed, and no longer did the U.S. Government offer a deferment for shipbuilding. I was to be officially inducted on May 3, 1943, at the age of nineteen.

On the day of induction, I was bused to Philadelphia, Pennsylvania, to be processed. As soon as I arrived, I was given a physical and then asked to fill out general paperwork and take an aptitude test. After several hours of this induction process, the guys who passed were lined up and their names were confirmed. As soon as they confirmed who you were, the military officers looked over long lists of papers. Then they would tell you where you were going and how you would get there.

When I got close to the front of the line, two navy guys who looked like officers came up to me, pulled me out of line, and requested that I follow them. I went with them to a separate area, where I was told that I was going to be drafted into the navy, not the army, and that I would be heading to a navy base for my basic training. They then loaded me on a bus headed to Maryland, where I would begin my basic training.

I did not know it at the time, but those navy officers had handpicked me so I could be trained as a Motor Machinist Mate to serve in the engine room of an LCT (Landing Craft Tank) that would be used in the upcoming D-Day invasion. The navy was looking for men with a mechanical background to be further trained to repair diesel engines and do mechanical maintenance of all types onboard the LCTs. My aptitude test, my experience working at the local filling station, my trade school training, and my experience as a welder indicated that I was an ideal candidate. Beyond the mechanical experience, they were looking for men who were shorter in height, smaller in stature, and lighter in weight to work in the tight quarters of the LCT engine rooms. Standing at 5'8" and just under 155 pounds, I certainly fit that bill.

When I arrived in Maryland for basic training, the first order of business addressed was haircuts, and in short order my hair was buzzed away. The next order of the day was for everyone to strip down to their shorts and file into a long line to get our medical inoculations. I hated getting shots and we all had to get several in each arm. When we came out of the shot line, we were in one big room that had long lines snaking around for each of the induction tests that followed. The room was cold and filled with an awful stench of body odor. It had the musky smell of a gym locker room made more pungent by nerves and anxiety. We were fingerprinted and then we gave blood and urine samples before being examined thoroughly.

We were issued "dog tags" with some basic information on them. Mine indicated my navy identification number, my blood type, and that I was Catholic. The tags were primarily for identification in the event I was killed or wounded. For the duration of my time in the service, I wore these tags every day and night attached to a chain around my neck. They served as a reminder that should I not make it home, my identity would be reduced to just another number in a death statistic. With that in mind, I signed up for a free ten-thousand dollar life insurance policy, to be paid to my father if I died while in the service.

Finally, we were directed to line up in the parade yard. Once there, we were made to stand at attention. The Petty Officer stood in front of the group, preparing to make his first address. He looked around at all of us and then asked, "Does any man here know how to stoke a coal furnace?" I raised my hand. He looked at me and said, "Okay, good." Then he told me to follow a young seaman who was graduating from boot camp that week and moving on to his next training.

I went with this seaman to the rear of one of the Quonset huts. He explained how the coal furnaces worked and showed me where the tools and coal buckets were stored. He showed me the coal storage and gave me the information needed when calling for more coal deliveries. Finally, he explained that there were seventeen Quonset huts to take care of, twenty-four hours a day, for the next twelve weeks.

He looked at me, smiled, then said, "You've got it made, man. For the next twelve weeks, those other poor bastards will be doing push-ups, marching, and running five mile drills, rain or shine, while you're here tending the Quonset hut furnaces. At the end of all this, you'll get to graduate along with them without killing yourself, and then move on to your next school just like the rest of them. Good luck, my friend."

That's just how it went. I stoked furnaces twenty-four hours a day. I would stoke, then sleep … stoke, then sleep. I showered during the day and ate in the mess hall on off-hours. I kept a low profile and did my job.

I set up my work quarters in a furnace room that had a larger window than most of the other Quonset huts; the view from there allowed me to see what was happening outside in the camp. During my idle time, I would sit on a large wooden table with my back against the wall and watch.

There were hundreds of men doing push-ups, jumping jacks, and sit-ups. I would see the Petty Officers standing face-to-face with seamen, yelling at them through red faces and forcing them to drop and do pushups. Other groups would be marching and learning to shoulder rifles up and down, spinning them and then standing at attention. At the same time, other groups would return from running several miles; they were often dirty and covered with mud. Sometimes they would run and work those fellows sixteen to eighteen hours a day. I saw guys that looked so exhausted, you would think they were going to collapse.

After twelve weeks of stoking furnaces, I graduated from basic training without one day of marching, running, or exercising. My final duty at basic training was to show the next coal furnace "volunteer" how to tend to the seventeen Quonset hut furnaces.

After basic training in Maryland, I was bused to Richmond, Virginia, where I took seven weeks of training in Diesel Mechanics, followed by eight weeks of Advanced Diesel Mechanics. I did very well in this training and scored the highest marks in both schools.

Upon finishing those two schools, I was moved to Norfolk, Virginia, where I received my amphibious training on LCTs. The United States military was preparing us for the upcoming assault of Europe. At several shipyards across the country, well over a thousand LCTs were being built for the upcoming D-Day assault, which was more than a year away.

As a seaman in the Amphibious Corps, I was trained in all the duties I needed to qualify as a Motor Machinist Mate on the LCT Mark 5 and the LCT Mark 6. I learned a great many things, including how to operate and maintain diesel and gasoline engines. I also learned how to run a variety of systems and equipment on the ship as well as how to read the tachometers and fill out the engineer's daily log book. In addition, some cross-training was required with the ship's electrician, front ramp operator, the helmsmen, and the pilot. When we were in general quarters, which was a condition of readiness for combat, I had to be in the ship's pilothouse adjusting the throttles of the three diesel engines to provide the required speed ordered by "the Conn," the Ensign. When at retrieval, it was my duty to stop, reverse, and idle the engines, as well as to operate the ship's anchor. While at my station in the pilothouse, I was required and trained to identify allied and enemy aircraft and ships.

Finally, there were physical qualifications for the ship's Motor Machinist. First, good eyesight was required—without glasses. Second, the navy wanted men of average to smaller size who were physically strong.

If we had those physical qualifications, along with our other training, then we qualified for working in confined spaces within the engine rooms and to man our duties at general quarters and we became Motor Machinist Mates. Growing up, I was always a few inches shorter than most of my peers. Now it was finally clear why I was pulled out of that army draft line and instead drafted into the navy.

With my amphibious training completed, I was ready for my first duty assignment. My orders were to report as a Motor Machinist Mate's assistant aboard an older freighter that would carry ammunitions to England. When I got to England, I would be assigned to LCT 9134.

Upon setting foot on the freighter, I was set up in the crew's quarters and given a tour of the ship as it was being loaded with ammunitions. It was built with two thinner steel hulls, one inside of the other. The inside hull was about a foot smaller than the outside hull. This created a twelve-inch space in between the two hulls that was filled with concrete. It truly was a concrete ship with one steel skin on the outside and another on the inside. I had never seen anything like this when I was working in the shipyards.

My first assignment was to operate and maintain the ship's distillers. The distillers were the units that took on seawater, removed the salt, and purified the water for drinking and all other domestic uses, such as showering and laundry.

A few of us sailors were afraid that our ship would be a target for German submarines. Little did we know that by this time in the war it was fairly safe to cross the Atlantic. The United States now had a huge fleet presence in the Atlantic, so attacks on ships carrying supplies to England were few and far between.

We started our trip across the North Atlantic in fairly heavy seas that progressively got worse. Within a matter of hours, Mother Nature went from gently rocking us to violently lurching our ship back and forth in the deep swells of the ocean. In the middle of the second night of the storm, we experienced the most severe weather of all—a gale that brought with it an unusual amount of thunder and lightning, periods of hail, and sixty miles-per-hour winds that were capable of knocking a full-grown man onto his back.

This North Atlantic storm batted us around violently. The ship began to pitch and roll heavily as the gale increased in intensity. My bunk was in the stern of that huge ship, meaning I was getting the brunt of the ship's nauseating movements. It felt like a never-ending elevator ride; we would go up, up, and up, then drop so fast it felt like we were going to fall out of our bunks. Actually, that would have been hard to do because there was only about two feet between the bunks, and they were wedged in tightly within the equipment. As the movement of the ship became greater, some men loosened the strings that held the canvas pad to the pipe frame. That made them sink down further in the bunk to ensure they would not roll out into the aisle.

I was in my bunk in the crew's quarters when an old Chief came in and said, "Everybody that has anything to do with engineering, get up and dressed now!" Turning to me, he said, "You're a welder, right?"

"Yes," I answered.

"Good, come with me."

With no delay we went to a large room near the middle of the ship at an intermediate level somewhere below the main deck. Water was weeping in through a crack in the hull. The old Chief said, "We're starting to break up. Water from the storm started coming through this crack a few decks up an hour or so ago. Now this crack is down to here, and the water is really starting to blow through it. If we don't do something soon, it's not going to be long until it gets below the waterline and this ship starts flooding and then breaks in half. We're going to start welding turnbuckles along this crack and start pulling this ship back together. A welding machine will be here in a few minutes along with the turnbuckles. The crews that bring you this equipment will stay here and assist you with this process. While you're welding in here, we'll also set up welders on other levels doing the same thing."

I welded for hours, all night long and into the next morning, knowing that by saving that old overloaded ship, we welders were saving our own lives and the lives of everyone on board. The next day when we were done, the old Chief literally gave us a pat on the back then turned and walked away. He didn't say anything, no real thanks, but that pat on the back was his way of saying, "Good job, men." We finished our trip to England and delivered our cargo to Portland Harbor.

When I got off that old freighter, I was told that I only had a short distance to travel to the mooring where I would find my next duty assignment, which was on board LCT 9134, a Mark 5 Landing Craft Tank.

I was directed to a dock and told to meet my next commanding officer, Ensign Thomas Corker, who was on board LCT 9134. When I got there, Corker—later and always to be known to me and the rest of the crew as "Corky"—and a few of the crew were already there.

The first duty for the crew during this time was to fit up the boat with tools and equipment. After that was complete, Corky had me go over all the engines, the ship's generators, the anchor system, and all the auxiliary equipment. In order to do my job properly, I needed to know this ship forward, backwards, and inside out.

Within a few days, all twelve of our new crew were aboard and getting to know each other. One of the new fellows was a guy from Philadelphia, a real talker and the biggest joker of the bunch. His name was Tillins, and the only thing bigger than his jovial personality was his height—he stood a lanky 6' 6". It was comical seeing him hunch over to avoid hitting his forehead on the tops of the low-hanging doorways. His assignment on board was to assist me with all my duties. When we were at general quarters or at our battle stations, Tillins was the front-ramp operator. Those few weeks spent working together quickly turned us into the best of friends.

LCT 9134 was then scheduled to have an "(A)" added behind the number "9134," meaning it had extra armored steel plates added to the pilothouse, the crews' quarters, and some other key areas. Early in 1944 we sailed 9134 from Portland to a shipyard near London to have our craft refitted with this armor plate. We were thankful to be on a boat with extra armor plate, not knowing at the time that it meant we would one day be in a situation that truly required the extra armor steel plating.

As a crew, we started our training together at a U.S. Navy base in Scotland. We first took 9134(A) out to sea and started getting familiar with its operation. Next we ran 9134(A) up on several sandy beaches, practicing landings. I would drop the anchor about three hundred yards out at sea as we ran toward the beaches and then bellied out our ship on the soft sand. Immediately another crewman would then drop our front ramp as if we were going to unload tanks. Next, while raising the ramp, we'd pull ourselves off the beach by retrieving our huge anchor.

As we became more confident with our ship, we ran through some exercises loaded with tanks to get familiar with the LCT's operation when loaded. Next we started to run maneuvers with one or two other landing craft. Finally, we were ready for practicing for the upcoming D-Day landings. The crew would take their assigned positions wearing helmets and full battle gear at general quarters or in full battle-ready mode.

As the Motor Machinist Mate, I was in the back of the pilothouse when I was at general quarters. I would run the three engines from there, controlling the throttles and the clutch for the LCT as our Ensign would order. The anchor could be dropped from there as we approached the beach and then retracted when it was time to be pulled off the beach.

As we began practicing for our landings, I stood on the right side of the pilothouse at the engine controls. The pilot or helmsman was in the front and center at the ship's wheel, and Ensign Corker stood to the left side of the pilothouse.

In full practicing mode, fully loaded with tanks and half-tracks, we hit the practice beaches side by side with other LCTs, dropped our ramps, unloaded, and quickly pulled our anchors in, pulling ourselves off the beach. Believe me, operating that flat bottom ship fully loaded was difficult, to say the least. Then we would sail out to larger ships and reload our LCT with more equipment and tanks and return to the beaches to unload again. Later during our training we began practicing a new technique. We started dropping floating DD tanks directly into the ocean. We did both these operations day in and day out for weeks as we prepared for the real thing.

One night, a few weeks before D-Day, there was a disaster. We were told that some of the LCTs that were practicing were attacked near England by German E-boats—the German equivalent of the U.S. PT boat.

The Germans had come across the English Channel and were attacking our practicing LCTs under the cover of darkness, firing several torpedoes and sinking one unsuspecting LCT. They had also hit a second LCT, setting it on fire with a direct torpedo hit that illuminated the dark of night with a fiery red glow. The enemy crafts strafed the decks of other LCTs with machine gun fire. We learned that as quickly as the attack had started, it had ended, as the German E-boats ran back to France before we could respond. After that attack, security became a lot tougher. No one had ever expected the Germans to cross the English Channel and attack a military exercise on England's coast.

Over the next several weeks, we continued to practice, and we all became very good at our jobs. By the time D-Day was at hand, we were experts at our upcoming duties. Little did we know that it still wouldn't be nearly enough to prepare us for the impending devastation.

[CHAPTER 2]

Landing at Omaha

On June 4, 1944, we left Portland Harbor. This time we could tell it was different than on previous trips out of the harbor. If it were just another practice, only a few groups of ships would be moving out to perform exercises. It had to be the real thing. Every landing craft and ship was completely loaded; people were moving everywhere. Trucks filled with supplies were backed up on every road near the harbor front, and traffic everywhere was heavier than usual.

We were fully loaded with one DD tank dozer, two Sherman DD tanks, and two half-tracks, as well as all the soldiers that manned this equipment. The overall plan was that all LCTs loaded for the D-Day initial assault would drop their tanks into the water about two or three miles out to sea. These swimming DD tanks were equipped with flotation equipment so they would float like a ship. They had two propellers and a rudder installed in the rear of the tanks to propel them to shore. For the upcoming invasion, we were scheduled to drop our tanks into the sea one hour before H-hour.

Our assignment was to drop our three DD tanks at sea an hour ahead of the first troops. Then an hour later, at H-hour, we would land on the beach with the two demolition crews in the half-tracks. The main job for the tank dozer, along with the two demolition crews, would be clearing the beach of obstacles. Working together, the DD tank dozer and two demolition crews would clear paths while the other two DDs provided protection for them. Additionally, all three tanks would later protect the troops as they stormed the beaches and moved inland. During the remainder of D-Day, it was planned that we would continue our duties by delivering Sherman deep-wading tanks directly to the beach for the continued support of our troops moving inland.

Our flotilla was called the Gunfire Support Group. We had those extra-armored LCTs because our assignment included landing on the beaches at Omaha. Now the crew was beginning to think all of that "extra" armor was not such a good thing to have after all.

We spent all of the daylight hours of June 4 cruising back and forth in the English Channel, only to be told that the seas were too rough for the invasion to take place on the morning of June 5. We thought we were going to continue cruising at least another full day as we waited for our official command to proceed.

Those flat-bottom LCTs had no keel under them. When fully loaded, they were hard to control. As we were cruising back and forth just outside the harbor during the evening of June 5, the winds were picking up, the weather conditions were getting rougher, and the seas were getting higher. Then, as we were making a 180-degree turnaround in those very high seas, waves began breaking over the side of the LCT, and water was running down into the engine room. The bilge pumps started pumping out water. We called for extra pumps, which were brought out to us to help pump water off the ship as quickly as possible. With high seas and the hundreds of tons of tanks and equipment we had on board, there was a chance we could sink if we took on too much water.

After we pumped out the boat and were back up to full-running ability, we continued circling in the ocean. I remember getting little sleep during the night of June 5 into the early morning of June 6. Unfortunately, before I was fully rested we were all called to general quarters. I took my spot in the pilothouse with the pilot and Ensign Corker. Corky told me this was the real thing. We had been given the command to go.

When we were finally fully out to sea and heading for France, we lined up in an organized fashion to make our way across the English Channel.

The open seas were even rougher, and our ship was being tossed all over the place, as were the contents of every man's stomach on board. Whether it was the tossing of the sea or nervousness about the upcoming battle, most of the army guys on board were getting seasick and heaving their dinner over the side of the LCT.

It must have been around 2:00 a.m. when Corky briefed the crew on our mission and informed us of our point of landing. He called the beach we were headed to Omaha Beach, and our sector was called "Dog Green." As we continued cruising in a line of LCTs across the English Channel, all of the sailors and the army guys became more and more quiet as we all started to feel the reality of what was ahead of us.

We were surrounded by other ships. The minesweepers ahead of our armada of warships had just completed opening the corridors that our task force would travel through as we made our way across the Channel to France. As I remember it, there was a thick haze of chilly moisture-laden fog that softly settled over the rough ocean on this unusually bright full-moon night. We were all amazed at the number of ships making the voyage with us. The scale of the operation was similar to nothing else in the history of the human race.

Small midget submarines, called "X-boats," had been lying submerged on the sea floor off the coast of Normandy, France. They rose to the surface in the early morning hours of D-Day, shining bright beacons whose light led all of our ships to assigned staging points.

When we were coming to our staging point about four or five miles offshore, hundreds and hundreds of airplanes were flying inland—so many that Corky commented, "My God, look at that … the sky is black with planes." Those bombers were heading toward France to make bombing runs over the beaches of Normandy. As they dropped their payloads, our eyes caught the flashes of the explosions seconds before our ears confirmed the sounds of devastation. As we continued to watch wave after wave of planes fly across the sky and bombing the coast, we told each other those bombs should soften the Germans up, and we hoped that they knocked out some of the bigger enemy guns guarding the beaches.

As we were moving into our final staging position, we passed several ships. We then heard the surreal sound of a bugle blowing the theme for "Charge."

Those on board looked at each other with puzzled expressions, when suddenly the battleship next to us emitted the sound of BOOM! BOOM! BOOM! as it fired its big guns. There were huge flashes, and the noise was absolutely deafening. When the concussion from the blast hit the surface of the water, a drenching, wet haze lifted off the ocean and spread for hundreds of yards, followed by smoke that was black and orange, with a unique and pungent smell of its own. Continually following those ear-splitting, thunderous blasts, huge wakes of water from the rocking battleship tossed our craft from side to side like it was a rowboat in a storm. Corky hollered, "Move us away from that ship as quick as you can!" I hit the throttles, and the pilot turned us to the west as we pulled away from the battleship before it fired again. It was the USS Texas that had just fired a salvo with its 14-inch guns toward the shoreline near the area at which we were to land.

It was the beginning of a naval bombardment that lasted for about an hour. Battleships up and down the whole coast were firing inland. An incredible amount of ordnance had been fired at the German strongholds that night. Huge flashes of light continued to fill the skies, clouds of smoke formed over the ships that were firing. It looked like a line of thunder and lightning running up and down the coast for miles. When the guns on the USS Texas fired, we could literally see the shells streaking through the sky, heading toward the beaches.

As Corky and I watched, we kept reassuring each other that no person or structure could survive that bombardment. We nervously tried to convince each other that our troops' impending landing would be pretty easy after all. In addition to the bombers hitting from the air and the hour-long bombardment from the battleships on the sea, eight special LCTs moved up, equipped with rocket launchers. When they commenced firing, it looked like thousands of rockets were launched in a few minutes. This was the final of the three bombardments. Our whole crew was now convinced that our air corps and navy had knocked the hell out of the Germans' shore defenses. We felt optimistic that our troops' landing would be fairly safe.

It was 5:00 a.m., an hour before H-hour, and we were lined up and ready to make our run toward our drop position about two or three miles off Omaha. The seas were somewhat calmer than they had been for several days, but Mother Nature was still proving to be unkind. Waves five-to-six-feet high caused the first twenty-seven out of twenty-nine swimming DD tanks that were dropped into the ocean on the eastern side of Omaha Beaches to sink like stones. This was a crisis. Vital equipment imperative for the success of the invasion was sinking to the bottom of the ocean, and with them the lives of many good men undeserving of such a worthless death.

Immediately, both the lower-ranking navy and army commanders onboard the LCTs wisely decided that the seas were much too rough to continue launching DDs into the ocean just to see them sink. They ordered that the remaining LCTs would not drop their tanks at sea but would instead take their tanks directly to the beach. This was a decision that seemed to me to be made on the spot, as the remaining LCTs on the western side of Omaha were immediately ordered to transport their tanks directly to the beaches.

The LCTs were quickly readied to now lead the assault ashore and land their tanks and demolition crews in the half-tracks ahead of the oncoming foot soldiers. These men would be the first troops to set foot on the beach ahead of the main assault, clearing obstacles for the oncoming troops. *These brave men would truly be the first troops on the beaches of Omaha.* Command knew that getting our main troops off the beach rapidly and taking the fight inland quickly would be key to establishing a solid foothold in France. It was intended that these first tanks and demolition crews landing ahead of H-hour would prepare the beaches for that quick push inland.

At about 6:00 a.m., we were given the signal to go and headed toward the Dog Green sector of Omaha Beach. Corky's eyes nervously scanned the horizon out the front windows of the pilothouse as we headed into the wind and rough seas alongside several other LCTs. I was tending to the throttles and reading the gauges when Corky hollered, "We got trouble!"

I looked out one of the front portholes and could see tracers streaking from the German machine guns as they fired at our lead LCTs. As bullets started ricocheting off the hull of our LCT, I realized this was the first time I had ever been under fire. It was also the first time any of our crew had ever been under fire or seen action.

As if to drive that fact home, artillery shells fired from behind the beach started exploding around us now that we were in range. Streaks of red filled the sky from the oncoming shells heading our way, and we watched them exploding as they made impact with the surface of the water.

Suddenly, one of the LCTs to the left of us exploded into a blaze of fire and smoke from a direct hit, splitting in half and sinking in moments. That was the first LCT we saw lose all of its tanks, men, and equipment to the bottom of the sea. Within a few moments, another explosion rocked us as a second LCT hit a mine, quickly rolling over and sinking, taking more men and equipment to the bottom of the ocean. With all the death and devastation around me, I became extremely scared and wondered what would happen to us. Would we be sunk as well? As we got closer to the beach, we heard an enormous amount of machine gun fire. Tracers flew through the air everywhere. Mortar shells exploded at the water's edge. An 88-millimeter gun located in the bunker directly ahead of us opened up and started firing at landing craft out at sea. I could see survivors from the lost LCTs in the water, but we had been ordered to make no effort to rescue them, as there were other craft assigned to that duty. Our job at that time was to get our tank crews on the beach before our troops started their assault.

I don't know how the Germans survived the airplane bombing, the ships' bombardment, and the rockets, but somehow they did, and it was now very clear that our landing was going to be hot. I took it upon myself to go down on the main deck. As waves were hitting against the front of the LCT, and as water was spraying over the deck, I started yelling to the army guys, "Fire them up! Fire them up! When we hit the beach, you're going to unload those tanks fast, followed by those two half-tracks." We had all practiced this many times; they would know just what to do.

Next, I ran over to Tillins. I told him it was time for him to man the ramp controls. I said, "Start the Briggs and Stratton pony motor and be ready to drop the ramp when we hit the beach." He nodded affirmative when suddenly our LCT started to spin in a circle. I could only think the worst. Were we hit? Did we hit a mine? Running, I headed back to the pilothouse. As I entered, I could see the pilot hanging on the wheel, pulling it to one side, and shaking. He was too afraid to even look out the window. Corky looked at me and then at the pilot. Without a word I took the wheel, turned the ship around, and headed toward Dog Green—the worst area on Omaha Beach. It was directly in front of some very tough German strong points that lay at the bottom of the Vierville Draw.

As soon as we were again sailing toward the beach, I found myself fighting a stiff westerly wind. I was struggling to control the flat-bottom boat without a keel under it in the rough seas. As we crashed through large waves, I looked out ahead and could see two concrete bunkers on the beach. The first one housed an 88-millimeter anti-tank gun. The second one was fortified with a 50-caliber machine gun. From those bunkers, the Germans were firing out to sea on an angle from our right to our left. I could see they were targeting any LCT that crossed their path as it came into the shore. Rather than cross the path of those guns, I veered to the right into the stiff winds and headed toward the western part of the beach, very close to Charlie sector so those bastards couldn't get a clean shot at us.

After veering to the right to avoid having to cross the line of sight of the 88 and the machine gun next to it, I got ready to drop our anchor when we were around three hundred yards offshore. Just when I was getting ready to release the anchor, a bullet crashed through one of the windows and hit the clock hanging on the back wall of the pilothouse. Both Corky and I were shaken up at the closeness of the hit. Regardless, I throttled up the engines as we readied to make our final run to the beach. When I estimated we were at the three-hundred-yard mark, I finally pulled the lever that released the anchor into the sea.

At that very moment, I heard the report of a cannon firing. I looked out the broken front window to see what was going on. As soon as I got my face up to the window, another blast from a cannon rang out as I saw one of the DD tanks on our deck firing toward the beach. Then there was another explosion as the third DD tank fired. That was the beginning of a series of about ten or twelve wildly inaccurate shots fired toward the beach from the tanks sitting on our deck. After those extremely inaccurate shots, the tankers cannons ceased firing as they readied themselves to disembark.

As we were coming closer to the beach, I could see obstacles constructed of wooden poles with mines tied to the ends of them—concrete cones, slanted poles, coils of barbed wire, and steel frames that were designed to rip the bottoms out of boats. This was the reason we had come in at low tide, so that we could see the obstacles on the beach and avoid them as we landed our LCTs onto the open areas.

I started looking for a clear place to "belly out" and slide our flat bottom boat onto the sand. As I looked out at the beach, I could see artillery shells exploding, creating big plumes of sand and smoke on our section of the beach along the water's edge. Corky looked at me and said he figured the German artillery spotters were marking locations with each shot, so we decided not to land in a spot near a bomb crater, realizing that it could be a marked location. As I looked out the front windows of the pilothouse, I saw a place where no artillery shells or mortars had yet landed and adjusted our course accordingly. Corky looked at me and nodded in agreement.

We were the only boat in our immediate area and also the farthest-west LCT landing craft approaching for a landing on the Dog Green section of Omaha Beach. As we came onto the beach, we drew mortar fire along with heavy machine gun fire from several locations. I remember that as I looked up onto the hills above the beach, I could see where the machine gun fire came from only because of the tracers. I could not see any more than the streaks of bullets coming out of nowhere. The machine gunners and their crews were well dug in and camouflaged. The mortar fire also seemed to come out of nowhere. The Germans had apparently created pit-like bunkers in the ground behind the beach, from which they fired their mortars.

During this time, I could also see German soldiers on the far side of the beach lighting up oil drums and creating smoke as a screen. That smoke, combined with the smoke of the explosions and the burning grass on the hillside above the beach, created a thick blanket of haze over the entire area.

Now I was only moments away from landing our ship in our designated area. With only a few yards left, Corky signaled Tillins, and then he signaled the army guys that it would be a couple of seconds until the front ramp would drop. We all felt the jolt of the boat hitting the sand as it slid onto the beach. After we slid for just a moment, we came to a sudden stop and, just like that, the LCT was no longer moving. When we were completely stopped, the reality of the mortar and artillery shells raining down and exploding on the beach was that much more present. At that second, the fear that raced through me was indescribable.

Tillins immediately dropped the ramp within a few seconds of our boat's landing on the beach. The first tank driver gunned his engine. The biggest piece of equipment, the tank dozer, jerked forward and straight away drove off the LCT. It immediately started heading toward the obstacles and barbed wire to begin creating openings. That tank dozer wasn't off the LCT but a few moments when I watched it get hit by a German 75MM cannon to the west of us. That 75 had fired from a bunker set in the hillside to our right and was positioned to fire down the length of the beach, parallel with the shore. As the tank dozer exploded, I could hear shrapnel from the exploding tank hitting the LCT. While heavy machine gun fire raged on and on, I didn't know it at the time, but I may have witnessed the death of the first soldiers to actually land on Omaha Beach.

From inside the armored pilothouse, Corky and I continued nervously watching out the LCT's windows. We could see mortars exploding on either side of us, and they were getting closer to the front of our LCT with each shot. When they exploded, we were bombarded with shrapnel as sand was thrown up over the front deck, covering us with clouds of smoke. Simultaneously, other mortar shells hit closer to the back and sides of us, throwing sheets of water up over us. Making matters worse were the large artillery shells, which were exploding within a few hundred yards, getting closer with each shot and creating an additional layer of haze over the beach. I could see the machine gun fire and their tracers as they were digging up sand on the beach then splashing across the water and hitting our boat. *I think it was at that moment I knew I was dead. I knew I would never see the end of this day. I would never again see home. I knew none of us would ever survive this beach.*

For a moment, I was frozen with terror and stood motionless, contemplating my death as I struggled to control my fear. I was standing there looking out at the beach, seeing explosions everywhere, when a huge flash to the east caught my attention. A mortar shell had just landed in the middle of one of our LCTs while it was unloading its tanks. When the smoke cleared a bit, I could see men fully engulfed in flames, jumping off the deck into the ocean to escape the blazing inferno. I looked away and said to myself, *Focus, focus, focus. Just do your job, focus on your job, do your duty.* I closed my eyes and shook my head and then looked up to see what was now happening on our boat.

By this time, the second tank on our LCT was shifting and moving forward. Squealing steel tracks moved forward on our deck as the tank lined up to exit down our ramp. Then down the ramp it went, passing the burning tank dozer and heading toward the enemy when, suddenly, it exploded as the first one had, hit by the same 75MM gun set up in that small hillside bunker to our west. They never even had time to fire a shot. Immediately following that explosion, our third tank went down our ramp and quickly turned left as it hit the bottom of the ramp, wisely retreating into the ocean. That third tank could lay back and hide from the Germans' 75MM gun firing down the length of the beach. When the tank was as deep into the water as it could get, our men started firing their cannon at the German bunkers and their machine gun at the banks ahead of us.

Now only the two half-tracks remained on our deck. As soon as the ramp was again clear, both vehicles went across the deck and headed down the ramp. The half-tracks could not retreat into the ocean like the third tank. Immediately they were under heavy machine gun fire. It wasn't long until the 75MM gun firing down the length of the beach also started firing at them. I saw an explosion from a miss and then within a few moments the first half-track exploded. I could see parts flying through the air, some even landing on our deck. As the second half-track tried to avoid that 75MM gun by turning and running to the east of our position, it was overwhelmed by machine gun fire. As soon as it stalled and came to a stop, the 75MM hit it. It exploded and immediately started burning. Both of the half-tracks were knocked out fairly quickly. None of the men in the demolition crews survived.

For a short moment, I once again just stood there, staring at the beach. The noise was deafening and the sound of bullets zipping past and mortars exploding around us rang in my ears. Machine gun fire was hitting our hull everywhere as the Germans tried to take advantage of any weak spots in our armor. Explosions from artillery and mortars rained down on all four sides of us. The artillery shells that were landing within a few hundred yards were making a shrill, squealing sound, followed by the sound of a blast. The explosions farther down the beach sounded more like thunder echoing at a distance. After a few more seconds of just staring at the beach, I heard Corky say to me, "We're now unloaded; it's time to get the hell out of here. Now it's our job to save this boat."

The mortar explosions were hitting even closer to us. The shrapnel from the mortars was starting to hit the sides of our boat hard, leaving the LCT riddled with deep pockmarks. I figured the Germans firing the mortars were zeroing in on us, as they were getting closer with each shot.

Corky and I were the only ones in the pilothouse. Tillins was up front inside the ramp control room. During the time we were unloading, Corky had directed the rest of our crew to take cover in the armored crew's quarters below. Corky and I both looked to the front of the LCT to the ramp control room where Tillins was standing. We were looking to see if the ramp was raising. It was not. I said to myself, "Come on, Tillins, let's go. Get that ramp up. Let's go! Come on, Tillins, you have to know we're empty. Raise that ramp. Come on, Tillins, let's go! If you would just look out at the deck you would see that we're empty. Let's go!" The ramp didn't move. What the hell was Tillins doing? I put my face up to a broken window in the pilothouse and hollered, "Tillins, raise the goddamn ramp! Raise the goddamn ramp! Tillins, raise the goddamn ramp!" But there was no way he could hear me. Yelling wasn't going to do any good at all—a person two feet away could not have heard anything over all of the noise from the explosions and the gunfire surrounding us.

With that, Corky turned to me and said, "Bill, you have to do something here." *Me?* I thought to myself. *What the hell does he think I should do? Goddamn it, how did it become my job to do something? He should just wait a goddamn minute; I'm the Motor Machinist Mate. Wasn't there some other son-of-bitch on this goddamn boat whose job it was to do something?*

Just as I was saying all this to myself, we took a major hit from a mortar shell. Corky and I both dropped to our hands and knees. I could feel the concussion and see the flash from the blast come through the broken windows of the pilothouse. I thought to myself, *Oh no, this is it. We're hit! Now for sure we aren't getting off this beach. We're definitely dead now.*

I figured the Germans had finally zeroed in on us and for sure they would now drop a mortar right in the middle of our ship. Corky and I got back up and looked out the windows. We could see that a mortar had hit the right side of our ramp, which was still down. It wasn't good, but at least it wasn't over yet.

Corky looked toward me again and said, "Bill, you have to do something here."

I thought to myself, *Goddamn, this is bad and getting worse every minute.* Corky and I both realized pulling off the beach with the ramp dragging in the sand would be difficult, if not impossible. If we did get off the beach with the ramp down, going backwards would be very slow, and controlling that flat-bottom boat without a keel would be impossible in those rough seas. Another problem would be trying to go forward with the ramp down. The ramp would dig into the water, flooding the deck and drawing the front of the LCT down until it had our boat standing on its nose with the back end of the craft lifting out of the water. We would need to get that ramp raised if we were going to get the hell out of there.

Corky told me that I was going to have to go up front and see why Tillins wasn't raising the ramp. He said he figured Tillins was most likely dead or that maybe the Briggs and Stratton engine that raised the ramp had been damaged from shrapnel. Whatever the problem was, we weren't leaving there until the ramp was raised. After thinking about it for a moment, I realized Corky was right to send me. If it was an engine problem or some other kind of mechanical problem, I was the Motor Machinist Mate and the best suited crewman for making quick repairs. Like it or not, I had no choice but to follow Corky's orders and go see what the problem was in the ramp control room.

I dropped down through a hatch in the floor of the pilothouse, which put me on a ladder going down into the crew's quarters. The crew's quarters was on the same level as the main deck. This was where Corky had earlier directed the crew to retreat to during our initial assault to avoid the heavy machine gun fire. They were glad to be in there, knowing it was armored and the only safe place to be under these conditions. When I came down the ladder, I saw them all huddled together against the front wall. Their faces told me they were just as scared as I was.

I cracked open the door to the main deck. If I was going to get the ramp up, I would have to make a run of about seventy-five feet to the ramp control room up front. Between the sound of the explosions of mortars and bombs, I could hear bullets hitting the LCT. I didn't want to run across that deck, but I knew if we didn't get the ramp up, we all were going to die there.

I shook the electrician's mate next to me. He had been huddled against the wall with the rest of the crew. I screamed in his ear, "When I go out that door, don't close it. I'm coming back in a minute and I don't want to have to stop and unlock the door." He nodded his head and told me it would be open just a little but not latched. I stood inside the door, looking out into hell for about thirty seconds. As I mentally prepared to go out on deck, I heard the sound of bullets ricocheting off steel. There were large splashes of sea water hurling across the deck from the mortar fire and artillery shells that were exploding as they impacted the ocean. After taking a few deep breaths, I opened the door and started running across the deck, praying to God that those few breaths wouldn't be my last. I didn't run two yards before I heard the BIZ! BIZ! BIZ! of bullets whizzing by me. I was so concentrated on the door I was running toward, I didn't even see the tracers from the machine gun fire. While running, it felt like buckets of water were being thrown at me across the deck. I could hear shrapnel hitting hard off the sides of our hull. When I got to the ramp control room, I ran right full speed through the open door and bounced hard off the inside wall.

It took me a few seconds to regain my senses, then I looked around and saw Tillins standing motionless in front of the Briggs and Stratton engine that raised the ramp. I was surprised to see he was still alive. I hollered, "Tillins, raise the ramp!" He didn't move. I grabbed him by the shoulders and hollered into his ear, "Raise the ramp; raise the ramp!" He still didn't move, so I shook him and got no response. He was frozen with fear. He couldn't move. I felt him shaking. I tried to pull him away from the ramp clutch handle so I could raise the ramp myself, but he was hanging on so tightly, I couldn't move him away. I tried to pry his hands free, but I couldn't break his grip or him. I grabbed his hands with mine, but there was no way to break his grip. Goddamn it, there was no time to waste! I needed to get the ramp raised immediately! I looked around and grabbed a short piece of pipe and swung it like an ax, hitting Tillins across the wrist and breaking both of his hands free. With that, I dropped the pipe and pulled Tillins to the floor.

I grabbed the clutch handle and pulled it into gear. I managed to get the ramp part of the way up and then it jammed. I lowered it a little and then raised it again. It went a little higher than before, then jammed again. I figured the mortar shell that had hit us somehow damaged the ramp. I continued lowering it a little and then raising it again. Each time the ramp went up a little higher. I did this over and over until the ramp was above the water.

Now we could get the hell out of there before the Germans dropped a mortar shell right in the middle of our boat! I went to the ramp control room door and got ready to make the run back to the crew's quarters. I looked out to make sure the door was still open.

Before making that run across the deck, I stood at the door for about thirty seconds, looking out into that hell-storm of death. I could see Corky standing in the pilothouse, looking down at me through one of the broken portholes. He had a firm look of determination on his face. His mouth was tightly closed and he was slowly nodding his head up and down indicating *yes, yes, yes* … silently encouraging me. I took a deep breath and started running. All I could think was how I hoped to live to make it to the door of our crew's quarters. Again, BIZ! BIZ! BIZ! as the bullets whizzed by me. Again water was hurling across the deck, and shrapnel was hitting off our hull. I had to stop at the end of the run to pull the door open and tripped and fell into the crew's quarters. The electrician's mate closed the door quickly. I got up as fast as I could and went directly up the ladder to the pilothouse. Corky got behind the ship's wheel as I headed for the winch controls.

It was time to pull in our anchor and get that goddamn boat the hell out of there. Before I could even get to the anchor winch controls, I heard another very close and huge explosion aft on the starboard quarter of the LCT. In the pilothouse we could feel the concussion and see the flash from the blast. As the boat shook and vibrated, I heard shrapnel hitting off the starboard quarter. Suddenly, I could hear the men below screaming, "Fire! Fire! Fire!" Smoke started coming up into the pilothouse from the hatch in the floor. It would be up to Corky and the crew below to take care of the fires. I had to get this goddamn LCT off this goddamn beach.

[CHAPTER 3]

Getting off the Beach

CORKY TOLD ME HE WAS going below to check on the crew that was fighting the fire and then to look over the ship to assess the overall damage. Were we still seaworthy? As he dropped below the hatch in the floor he said, "Start pulling us off this damn beach."

I reached for the anchor gearshift, shifted it into high gear, then eased the clutch into gear to start the high-speed anchor retrieve that would pull us off that God-forsaken beach. Nothing. The anchor did not start to retrieve! I disengaged it. Then I pulled the clutch into gear again. Still nothing. It didn't respond a second time. I disengaged and re-engaged it again. Still nothing. I shifted the anchor system into low gear, and I pulled the clutch and re-engaged it again. It started to retrieve in low speed. At least the system was still working, but we didn't have time to retract in low gear. Up to this point the German mortars had been inaccurate and were not all that consistent. God only knew how much longer it would be until a mortar made a direct hit to the middle of the deck. I disengaged the clutch, shifted back into high gear, and re-engaged it again, hoping that this time we would start to retrieve in high speed. Nothing. High gear was still dead.

In and out, in and out, in and out. Nothing. I shifted back into low gear a final time. I was getting more worried and afraid by the moment; we had already stayed here way too long. I jerked the clutch to re-engage into low gear one more time. Nothing. Now both low gear and high gear were not working. What the hell was wrong with the goddamn thing? Again I shifted and engaged in and out of high gear, and still nothing. I tried again in low gear. Nothing. The whole anchor winch system was dead, and soon our entire crew would end up the same if I couldn't get the goddamn thing working.

What the hell was I going to do? After a few seconds of thinking, I had an answer. I would go out on the deck and check the pony engine, the gearbox, and the cable and cable reel—the entire winch system—so I could analyze the problem.

There was no way I was going to go outside without first checking to see how intense the gunfire was at that point. I stood at one of the pilothouse windows looking out as I was thinking about going back into that hell a second time. As I looked out, I could see several other tanks and vehicles now burning on the beach. None of the tank crews or half-track crews of demolition specialists whose job it was to create an opening in the barbed wire and remove obstacles had survived this section of beach. There were no openings in the obstacles and nothing cleared for the soldiers who would soon be coming ashore. The 75MM to the west made it impossible for any equipment to advance across the beach. The only tanks that were not blown up were still hiding in the water and not moving ahead, due to the 75MM firing down the length of the beach. To our east I could see several other destroyed landing craft and tanks that had been hit by the 88 MM that was to our left, shooting out of its bunkers on a forty-five-degree angle toward the east.

The several LCTs that had successfully landed had quickly discharged their equipment, retracted, and were now gone. We were one of the few major targets left on the beach, and as a result were drawing heavy machine gun fire from several locations. Tracers were coming from several different angles, and I realized if I stepped out of the pilothouse, I'd be dead.

Bullets hit us like lead raindrops. I was getting more scared that the mortars or artillery fire would soon drop one of their bombs right on top of us. If that happened, a faulty anchor system was going be the least of our problems. This was bad; those Goddamn dirty dogs were going to get us after all. I just stood there looking out the window waiting to be blown off the beach. We were all dead for sure.

Suddenly the machine gun fire eased up. I looked out the window to see why and saw that the army's 29th Infantry Division was starting to land. Those men were the first foot soldiers coming onto shore in the Landing Craft Vehicles for Personnel, also known as "Higgins Boats." As these smaller landing craft came to shore five abreast, I could see the tracers from the machine guns begin to focus their fire on them instead of us. As I watched from the pilothouse, their ramps dropped and the soldiers in those boats started to assault the beach. As they exited their landing craft, I could see them being cut down almost immediately. Most of the men coming off of the LCVP fell dead within seconds, their bodies riddled with shrapnel and bullets. Only a few were able to find shelter behind the obstacles on the beach. Some men even started wading back into the water up to their necks.

As the enemy continued aiming their machine guns at the landing soldiers and not on us, I had the opportunity to go out on the deck and see if I could get the anchor system to retrieve. I went to the side door and opened it just a crack. Water was still splashing over the deck from exploding shells. Looking out the side door of the pilothouse, I began inspecting the entire anchor system. I couldn't see much of it from the doorway, which meant I would have to go out on deck and get a better look ... the sooner, the better. I took a deep breath, hoping it wasn't my last, and quickly ran through the door and out onto the deck, staying as low as I could. I dropped to my knees behind the equipment and started looking over the anchor winch system. As I was kneeling to examine it, water continuously splashed over me, making it tough to see what I was doing. I could see pockmarks everywhere from where bullets had hit. The noise level was deafening. After checking over the main drive gear, I made my way to the pony engine that powered the system. Dropping to my knees behind the engine, I started to examine it. It only took a moment to notice the fan blades weren't rotating. Immediately I realized that amidst all of the noise, I hadn't noticed that the engine wasn't running. Reaching for the starter, I cranked it over. It started right up.

Now we were back in business. I would later remember that it was me who had stalled the pony engine by disengaging and re-engaging the clutch and shifting back and forth into and out of high and low gear. It happened because I hadn't been able to hear the sound of the engine amidst the noise of explosions and machine gun fire. I had stalled the engine like a kid learning to drive a car with stick shift.

As soon as the pony engine was running, I made my way back into the pilothouse, closing the door behind me. My clothes were soaked and water was dripping down my face. I considered myself lucky just to have had an opportunity to get out onto the deck. Grabbing the gear shift, I pulled the anchor system into high gear and this time eased the clutch into gear, but the high-speed retrieve was still dead. I shifted into low gear and eased the clutch into gear; it started to retrieve in slow speed. I realized that low speed was the only speed we had left and that it would be better to retract in low gear than not at all.

With an incoming tide and a revived anchor winch system, there was a moment of hope: we might just get off of the beach before one of those goddamn mortar or artillery shells landed on us.

I tried to shake off my fear and exhaustion. I slowly exhaled and started to catch my breath as I dried my face with a rag. As we were now slowly pulling away, I again looked out the window to see what was happening on the beach. At that point, even the mortar and artillery fire were moving away from us and toward the soldiers landing on either side of our LCT. What I saw in those moments can only be described as hell on earth.

"I couldn't believe the devastation those soldiers were experiencing. With no exaggeration I can tell you that the water at the edge of the beach was red with blood. Men were lying dead and dying everywhere. Those that were still alive were trying to find cover behind the Germans' obstacles that were planted on the beach; they were also taking cover behind the blown-up equipment we had dropped there. Machine gun fire was tearing them to pieces. If a machine gun slowed and concentrated fire on one man, it would literally cut him in half. For those foot soldiers on the beach, moving forward must have seemed futile because of the lack of cover and the

rows of barbed wire blocking any advancement. Mortars and artillery fire were exploding everywhere, sending clouds of sand and smoke into the air. I could feel the concussion of the explosions from the closer mortars and artillery landing in our area of beach. When these exploded, I saw bodies of men both dead and still alive sent spinning into the air. The noise was so loud you couldn't hear yourself think. I saw soldiers screaming with fear. As I looked at the wounded on the beach, I could tell, even all the way from our pilothouse, that those men were in agony. I will never forget the desperate feelings I had on that day as I watched landing craft that were bringing troops to shore become targets and get hit by artillery shells and mortars. I cringed every time I saw one of them struck and then saw men in the water swimming for their lives next to the lifeless bodies that were floating everywhere. It was a God-awful scene to witness.

This was certainly the most horrible event I had ever seen up to that point in my life. Saving Private Ryan gets close to showing what that moment looked like, but it really doesn't reveal the overall sense of horror and the scope of devastation. In the movie they break out quickly and move up the beach. If you were there, you would know that was not how it actually happened. I saw several hundred men landing. I would guess that 75 percent of the very first wave of men I saw hit Dog Green and Charlie sector on Omaha Beach died in the first few minutes they were on the beach.

No movie can portray everything I experienced on that day. To experience the horror of seeing so much blood being spilt as you're watching machine gun tracers targeting and cutting down whole groups of men is something that can't be recreated in a movie. When you're watching a movie, you can't feel the concussion from exploding shells. You can't smell the ocean or feel cold salt water splashing over you and soaking your clothes. The extreme ear-splitting sounds from explosions and gunfire are excruciating, and the ringing in your ears can't be recreated in a movie—neither can bullets buzzing past you like fast-flying bumblebees.

In a movie, you can't smell the odor of cordite mixed with smoke. I remember the stench of all the smoke on the beach. There was smoke from exploding shells, smoke from several tanks and other vehicles that were burning across the beach, smoke from the surviving soldiers of the 29th creating a cover smoke to hide behind on a beach with no cover. There was also a black smoke coming from the drums of drain oil the Germans had burning for their cover on the beach, and white smoke from the burning grasses above the beach. The combined effect gave the whole place a unique odor I would never smell again for the rest of my life. All of these sensory assaults and the violence witnessed set a real veteran of Omaha apart from a movie actor.

I get a bit upset and certainly don't agree with how the Private Ryan movie depicts the DD tanks on Dog Green. Even people who know the opening scenes of the movie well don't appreciate this misconception. Early in the scene a soldier, referring to the obstacles on the beach, states: "I gotta clear these obstacles, make holes for the tanks." The character portrayed by Tom Hanks replies with "All the armor's floundering in the Channel," implying that the soldier's intended action would have been a waste of time. Later, when Tom Hanks is lying at the foot of the sea wall along the base of the Vierville Draw, he says to his radioman, "Shore party, no armor has made it ashore; we got no DD tanks on the beach. Dog One is not open." Finally, during the scene in which a mirror is stuck to a bayonet with chewing gum, it was disappointing to me to hear Tom Sizemore say (as he holds the bayonet and looks into the mirror), "It's a little defilade over there, but it's a perfect fire position if we could get some goddamn armor on the beach."

Hearing those words in those three movie scenes cut me like a knife. I guess the difference between them and me is that I was really there, and I know the navy had a lot of armor on the

Dog Green section of beach in front of the Vierville Draw. We landed three tanks, and I saw several other brave LCT crews drop off their tanks as well. I don't know how many tanks were knocked out, but I would guess that on the western side of Omaha, we landed thirty to forty tanks. Those tanks were the ones we carried directly to the beach before the brave soldiers of the 29th Infantry Division ever started their assault.

Tom Hanks and Steven Spielberg are truly fine professionals in that they did an overall magnificent job communicating the Omaha story, but both they and the movie's writers have their history wrong regarding the tanks at Vierville on Omaha Beach. What they failed to realize was that it was only on the eastern end of Omaha Beach that the first twenty-seven out of twenty-nine floating DD tanks from the 741st Tank Battalion sank because of the rough seas. Immediately after that travesty, the army officers on board the LCTs carrying the 743rd Tank Battalions changed their plans of launching the remaining DD tanks on the western end of the beach. They quickly communicated with the onboard naval officers commanding the LCTs of the change in their plans. I don't know that any official orders were ever given to either the army or navy officers on the LCTs. The change in plans seemed to be an on-the-spot decision. Regardless, the remaining LCTS changed their plans and decided not to drop their tanks at sea; instead, they carried the remaining first wave DD tanks directly to the beach ahead of the first wave of oncoming soldiers. It was because of this change in plans that there were many tanks on the western end of Normandy Beach, more specifically the Dog Green section of Omaha Beach in front of the Vierville Draw. Based on my personal experience, Tom Hanks' character was wrong. The armor at Vierville wasn't floundering in the Channel.

Having witnessed the events of D-Day firsthand, it is truly disappointing to me that the brave Tankers and our LCT crews that were truly the first soldiers to hit the Omaha beaches on D-Day had their stellar service described as "floundering" in the movie. Somehow the history of these courageous initial landings has been lost. It's truly unfortunate that we never see these men depicted as the first military troops to commence the opening assault on Omaha Beach. Honestly, it's nearly altogether forgotten that they were ever associated with the D-Day landings. They're never seen in old newsreels or photos, they're not shown in World War II documentaries, and there are no movies depicting them as the initial troops to assault the beaches. Unfortunately, their efforts are mostly unknown. It is as if the memories of their heroism drowned in the waves of Omaha.

You can't imagine and definitely can't film what you feel inside yourself when you are manning your post, knowing that any minute you're going to die. Believe me, it took everything I had to man my post. To experience fear on that level cannot be explained to another person. You can only experience that on your own. Saving Private Ryan gives a small taste of this experience, but truly doesn't capture the level of real fear you feel. Even fifty-four years later, I shake just talking about it.

Today some of those same feelings return when I hear the musical notes of "Taps." The fear instilled in me on June 6, 1944—those emotions of terror, anxiety, and distress—ripple through every nerve in my body when I hear a bugle play those sad notes. In a strange way, I revere and at the same time loathe those musical notes, as they make me remember that horrible day."

-Bill Grannetino, 1998

As I watched the horrible scene of the army's 29th Infantry Division being torn to pieces in real time, the LCT suddenly started to float. Our winch had finally pulled the LCT far enough out to sea, and I could feel the movement of the ocean. As we were retracting and getting more buoyant, the incoming tide was also helping us float.

I ran down to our tool storage to look for a cable cutter, hoping to cut the anchor cable now that we were buoyant. That way we wouldn't have to wait to completely retrieve the anchor. Not finding anything that would cut the thick steel cable, I realized that idea wasn't going to work.

As I was coming back into the pilothouse, Corky was just returning from checking on the crew and doing his inspection of the ship's overall damage. He had also felt the ship starting to float and had headed back to the pilothouse. As he came through the floor hatch he hollered, "Get this thing turned around and let's get the hell out of here." I immediately checked the gauges and saw that only one of our three engines was still running. Well, one engine would have to be enough to get us the hell out of there! With that I turned the engine's throttle up and got behind the ship's wheel, preparing to turn the boat around. It seemed to me that waiting to finish the remaining anchor retrieval took forever. Finally, when our anchor was in far enough, I turned the wheel hard and engaged the props. I was turning the LCT 180 degrees as fast as I could. Suddenly, there was an explosion on our port quarter as I rolled our stern around and into a ramped, wooden-log obstacle with a mine tied to it. Damnit! With the tide coming in, I didn't see it as I was swinging around! There was no way of telling how much damage it caused, so I gunned our remaining engine and started out to sea. When we caught up to our anchor, I slowed the boat and finished retrieving it. Then I turned to the open sea and gave the engine full throttle to get the hell out of there. When we got about a half a mile offshore, our pilot came up from below, returned to the ship's wheel, and took over again. Not a word was said; we just looked at each other and shook our heads. We had made it; we were off the beach, and it seemed our LCT was still seaworthy.

The time was around 7:00 a.m. I couldn't believe I was still alive! I couldn't believe any of us had lived through that. How we hadn't had a mortar or artillery shell land inside the boat was a miracle that I'll never understand. Goddamnit, that was awful. I was exhausted, both physically and mentally. I went out onto the upper deck to catch my breath and dry off. I was cold and wet, and the cool fifty-degree air sent shivers running throughout my body.

I looked down and saw Tillins coming out onto the lower deck from the hatch of the ramp control room. He was holding his wrist, which had swollen considerably and looked a painful shade of purplish-red. He looked at me and smiled, shaking his head. I hollered over, "Are you okay?" He laughed a little with that dumb look on his face and hollered back, "You know, Bill, a fellow could get killed around here!" We both laughed a little bit.

Then the electrician's mate came up from below. He hurried past us and went into the pilothouse and talked to Corky for a moment. Next thing, he and Corky had come out from the pilothouse and walked hurriedly over to Tillins and me. Corky asked, "Do you know we're taking on water in the engine room?"

"Must have been that mine we hit on that wooden log obstacle," I answered. Without any explanation, Corky said, "Get on this now. Get down there right away, check things out, and get it taken care of." Well, it seemed it was now my problem, since I was the Motor Machinist Mate and the engine room belonged to me. I turned to Tillins then turned my eyes toward the ship's ladder. Without a word, Tillins and I headed below.

In several locations around the LCT we had placed sledgehammers and several stacks of wooden wedges made of soft pine. The wooden wedges were about sixteen-to twenty- inches long. They were made round and were about four inches in diameter on one end and tapered to a point on the other end. Since they were made of soft pine, they could be driven tightly into a shrapnel hole in the hull by using sledgehammers. In the case of a larger hole or a misshaped hole, two or three wedges could be stacked together and driven tight to stop water from flooding the boat.

On our way to the engine room, Tillins and I grabbed a stack of wedges and a sledgehammer. When I got down into the engine room, I decided we needed to pump the room down to a lower level before plugging holes. The bilge pumps were already pumping and not keeping up, so I had some crew members help me set up the pumps we had used the other day when high seas were flooding us. After we had the extra pumps set up to aid the bilge pumps, we managed to get the water level low enough in the room to plug holes. Using the wooden wedges, we plugged several holes that were below the waterline, completely stopping the flow of water into the engine room.

It looked like the artillery shell that hit very close to our aft on the starboard side had sent several pieces of shrapnel through our hull above and below the waterline. This was the same exploding shell that had started the fire in the crew's quarters. I couldn't say how close it landed, but it was one hell of an explosion. I remember feeling the concussion from that blast and hearing shrapnel hitting hard off the starboard quarter. Now looking things over, I could see that same blast had severely damaged several components on two of our three engines, which put them out of commission. That explained why we only had one engine still operating.

On the port side, where we had hit the mine tied to the wooden log obstacle, there were only a few small holes to be plugged. That mine must have exploded as it hit the sand on the bottom of the ocean, as opposed to a direct impact with our hull.

As we finished up in the engine room, I could feel the ship slowing and stopping, then moving a little more, then slowing and stopping again. Time after time this happened. We headed back up onto the deck to see why we were stopping like this. Once back on the main deck, I saw guys from our crew reaching over the side and pulling men on board. They were pulling in guys who had been on landing craft that had sunk. This went on for a while, as there were a lot of men in the water to be rescued. It seemed that every time we picked up two or three guys, we would spot a few more. We would move our craft over to them, pick them up, and start all over again.

While we were pulling men out of the ocean, Tillins and I were trying to see what was happening on the shore. Over the whole beach we could see a low-hanging cloud of white smoke suspended over the shoreline, and a couple of the surviving tanks moving around and fighting on the beach. We could also see several tanks and vehicles that were not moving—apparently they had been knocked out of commission. At this distance we couldn't really see what the troops were doing, but we could definitely see the explosions from artillery shells and mortar fire. The LCVPs (which are the landing craft for soldiers) were still taking men ashore, and we could see others returning and heading back toward the ships out at sea.

Looking out to sea, we could see what looked like hundreds and hundreds of ships across the entire horizon. On the larger ship, we could see the small blimps tied to cables floating above them. These blimps were designed to keep enemy planes from dive bombing and dropping their bombs on decks. If an enemy plane targeted a ship, its wings would hit the cable holding the blimp. As we stood on the deck looking at those blimps flying high above the ships, we were again reminded of the magnitude of this operation. It was so absolutely enormous it was unbelievable.

It was around this time a smaller control vessel pulled up alongside our LCT to check if we had wounded on board that needed immediate care. Corky indicated we didn't have any severely wounded, and he was then informed that the landings in the area of the Vierville Draw were shortly going to be stopped because the troops in that section were so completely devastated.

While most of the crew was still helping pull soldiers out of the water, Tillins and I started looking around the ship to see the extent of the damage for ourselves. We first looked at the ramp. It was only partially closed, pretty well jammed, and certainly not aligned like it should have been. I figured at some point it would require some rather extensive repairs, but I was thankful that it was functional enough to get us off that damn beach.

I then heard Corky call to me. "Bill, go to the upper deck and start looking at the anchor system." I headed up and immediately saw that the electric controls that operated the anchor speed were damaged from machine gun fire or flying shrapnel. Now I knew why we had no high-speed anchor retrieve. Looking around further, I saw that paint was chipped everywhere, and dents and dings mottled every surface.

Tillins came up from the main deck and said he wanted me to see something. We went back down to the main deck and stood there.

"Do you feel that?" he asked. "Look at the front end. Does that look like it is lower than it should be? Also, doesn't our whole boat seem to be drafting extra deep in the water?"

I stood there looking and seeing how we were listing to the front and how deep we were drafting. Then it came to me. We might be taking on water in the front end, below the waterline. The mortar shell that had damaged our ramp could have blown a hole somewhere in the front of the hull. It soon became apparent to me that we were taking on water in our front end somewhere below deck.

As Corky was making his way around the boat checking on the crew, he walked up to us and asked what we had going on. I explained the situation to Corky. Without further discussion, he looked at me and said, "Get on it."

I didn't hesitate for a moment. I turned and told Tillins, "Get some men and let's get our extra pumps up front and start pumping." After a few minutes of staging equipment and setting up, we were pumping. As I watched the water level around the hull, I saw we were losing ground; the water was coming in faster than we could pump it out. We grabbed some more wooden wedges and a sledge hammer to plug some more holes, but the holes were so low on the hull we couldn't get to them from inside the boat.

Looking over the side, I wondered if we could get to the holes from outside the boat. That gave me an idea. I told Tillins to lower the ramp and I'd see if we could get to these holes by standing on the open ramp. Tillins went into the ramp control room and started the pony motor to lower the ramp. When he engaged the clutch, the ramp started down and then jammed. He raised it a little and lowered it again. It got a little lower the second time before it jammed again. Up and down, up and down, the ramp lowered a bit more each time. Finally, when the ramp had gotten down to almost level, I heard the sound of cracking steel. Before I could yell to Tillins to hold on, the right side of the ramp broke off of the right hinge and swung down into the water, cracking and breaking the left hinge, dropping the whole ramp into the ocean, and tearing it off the chains. It was gone in seconds. The mortar shot that had hit the ramp on the right side when we were on the beach had apparently done enough damage to the right hinge to now cause it to break completely. I could hardly believe it—our ramp was gone.

We were not only taking on water because of holes below the waterline, but we had also lost the boarding ramp. Without the ramp, we had no way of getting to the holes and driving wooden stakes into them. The boat was severely listing to the front.

We went up to see Corky. I told him that if we didn't do something pretty soon, we were going to start sinking. We talked about possibly going back to the fleet and getting some navy divers to plug the holes, but we decided it would take too long. If we went back to the fleet, we could sink before anyone could organize any kind of repairs, especially considering that we were still in the middle of the D-Day invasion. We were on our own. As

Corky and a couple of us talked about it, we decided we only had one choice, and that was to run the LCT back onto the beach so we could get below the waterline and plug the holes.

Corky and I discussed the best place to land—there were no ideal spots. To our west was all rock and cliffs. Straight ahead was our first landing location, and we both said, "The hell with that." To the east was miles of Omaha Beach. Guessing that we only had forty-five to sixty minutes before we started sinking, we headed east and back to Omaha.

As fortune would have it, we were lucky that earlier I couldn't find anything strong enough to cut through the anchor cable. We would need it again to pull ourselves off the beach a second time. Corky and I went to the pilothouse; Corky directed the pilot to turn the LCT toward the shore. I throttled up the engine. We started heading east, then the pilot turned us to the starboard and we started moving toward the shore.

Tillins went down on deck and started getting wooden wedges and a sledgehammer ready at the front of the LCT. The electrician's mate and I went to the shot-up electric box that controlled the winch speed and wired it direct for high-speed retrieve. This time when we were ready to get off the beach, it wouldn't be on slow retrieve.

When I was done helping the electrician's mate, I headed back into the pilothouse to tend to the engine and run the anchor system. As we were getting closer to the shoreline, the red streaks of artillery shells from miles behind the beach again started impacting the water around us, exploding just like they did on our first trip in. I throttled the engine up, getting ready to once again land on the beach. Being back in a hot area, the pilot again started shaking and hanging on to the wheel. Corky looked my way. I took over the wheel without a word being said as the pilot headed below.

With the tide in as far as it was, if we had landed 9134(A) anywhere close to our first location near Charlie Sector, we would have been a sitting duck for that 75MM on the cliff to the far west. With that in mind, I kept veering east, because there was no way we were going back to where we had landed the first time. From our present location, looking in toward the shoreline and a bit to the west, I could see the two angled concrete bunkers—the one that housed the 88MM firing out to sea on an angle from our right to our left, and the one housing the 50-caliber machine gun. They were still targeting any landing craft that crossed their path, which was the very area to where we were headed. When we got closer to the beach, I could see three LCTs that had been destroyed by that 88MM during the initial landing all sitting in a row. Across the beach in front of those devastated LCTs were several destroyed tanks that had been taken out by that 88. They were now being covered by the incoming tide.

On this trip in we would have no choice but to cross the path of both bunkers. As I was starting the final stage of our run in, Corky yelled over to me, "The tide is now in far enough that if you get us past that 88 without getting hit, they won't be able to target us that far in."

I started watching as the 88 fired so that I could determine how quickly they reloaded and fired again. As I counted seconds between shots, we were being sprayed by 50-caliber bullets as we passed the first bunker's line of fire. Then as we were coming closer to the line of fire of the 88MM, I slowed down and lay back for a moment. As soon as I saw the flash of the 88, I hit the throttle and quickly crossed its path before they could reload and fire their gun again. After crossing in front of those two bunkers and now out of their line of fire, it was full throttle into the shoreline.

When the time was right, I dropped the anchor into the ocean and watched as anchor cable started reeling off the back of our LCT. I looked for a clear spot to land the ship. As we were coming into the beach just off the shore, there were bodies floating everywhere, and I had to avoid several sunken Higgins Boats. I could again see the water breaking red from blood on the sand of the beach. The water nearer the beach had a blue-green coating on top because it was skimmed over with gas and diesel fuel from all the destroyed equipment that was leaking fuel into the ocean. A good bit of that fuel was leaking from an LCT that had been blown completely upside down at the edge of the beach. For the first several feet, the edge of the beach was covered with bodies. I could hear some machine gun fire in the distance, but not nearly what we had when we had been on Dog Green near Charlie Sector. The mortars and artillery shells were still exploding over much of the beach.

As I looked across the beach I could see that, in this section, the soldiers had cleared paths through many of the obstacles and were moving up the beach. Many were taking cover at the sea wall near the top of the beach.

Above them, other soldiers had reached the top of the bluffs and were flanking and engaging the German bunkers. The pathways up to those bunkers were covered with fallen soldiers.

With the tide much higher now, the steel obstacles and wooden poles with bombs tied on them became a real concern. I picked a spot that looked somewhat open. As I landed the flat bottom of the LCT on the sand, it dug in from all the weight of the water inside the hull. We stopped suddenly and pretty darn hard. I didn't know it at the time, but hitting the beach with all that water weight inside had buckled our hull.

As soon as we were completely stopped, Corky hollered, "Get on it." I rushed out of the pilothouse, dropped down one level, and ran across the main deck in a full sprint. Tillins was standing up front waiting for me. As I got to the front, I looked to see how deep the water was. After seeing sand beneath the waves, I jumped off the front of the LCT into about a foot and a half of water. Tillins handed me some wedges and the sledge hammer and followed me into the cold water. We ran around to the starboard bow and found three holes in the hull.

I could smell the gas and diesel fuel in the water, and it wasn't long until I could feel it burning my skin, especially where I had already started chaffing from running around the boat in wet clothes soaked by salt water. But I sure as hell didn't have time to worry about chaffing or burning skin.

Tillins got ready to plug up the holes by putting the first wooden wedge in line with the first hole. Tillins held the wedge, and I felt the concussion of an artillery shell explode at a distance behind me as I started driving the wood into the punctured hull. I drove it so tight, the wood took the shape of the holes. In the second, larger hole, we drove three stakes at one time. I alternated hitting each different stake in the bundle, again driving the softer pine wood into the shape of the shrapnel hole.

While driving these stakes, we felt a second concussion from another artillery shell exploding a little closer than the first one. *Goddamnit*, I thought, *they must have a spotter giving the artillery directions and they're walking artillery shells in on us. Son-of-a-bitch, we better hurry up here before the next artillery shot lands on top of us.*

Tillins then held several stakes up to the third and largest hole with both hands, and I began swinging the sledge hammer like a mad man, worried the next artillery shot would be the one to find its mark. When they were all good and tight, I dropped the sledge hammer into the water and we both crawled back on to the LCT, just as another artillery exploded closer than the one before. Time was sure as hell running out as we started running for the pilothouse.

As I was coming back into the pilothouse, Corky shouted, "Are we good to go?"

"Yes," I hollered as I took my place behind the controls. Immediately I pulled the anchor clutch into high gear and started reeling the anchor in, this time in high-speed retrieve, so we could quickly pull our LCT off that God-forsaken beach.

Then a fourth artillery shell hit even closer than the first three. I could hear the sounds of several pieces of shrapnel pinging off the hull. I looked over at Tillins, who was now manning the wheel. He looked back at me and said, "Damn good time to be getting the hell out of here."

It was only about one more minute until we were completely buoyant and the anchor was in. Tillins spun the ship's wheel and turned us around then headed us back out to sea. Again I had to watch as the angled 88 fired out to sea. I would again have to try to determine how quickly they reloaded and fired. As Tillins manned the wheel, I brought our LCT forward just short of the gun's line of fire. I slowed the engine before we crossed their line. As I had done before, as soon as I saw the flash of their gun, I hit the throttle and we ran across their line of fire. When we were beyond their line of fire, I expected the 50-caliber to open up on us, but they didn't. Looking out the pilothouse window, I could see that they were forcing their fire on a wave of incoming Higgins Boats and were no longer interested in us. Then it was full throttle out to sea.

When we were well out at sea, Corky started coordinating the crew's efforts and what each man was responsible to do. Tillins gave the wheel back to the pilot, and Corky sent both of us down to again start manning the pumps to get the boat floating higher in the water. While we were doing this, Corky ordered several of our crew to again start retrieving men from the water. I remember talking to one of those fellows we pulled out of the ocean. He said he had set out three times to land on the beach and he hadn't made it to the shore yet. He also told us he heard that the landings in the area of the Vierville Draw were again back in full swing. The top brass had decided no matter how bad the devastation at Vierville, the survivors still on the beach would not be abandoned.

It was at about that time we saw several navy destroyers coming in near the beach and paralleling the shoreline. They started firing point blank at the German bunkers in an effort to help the army's soldiers move up the beach. Huge explosions sent tons of concrete flying into the air. As we watched, we were amazed at how close to the beach these huge ships could get without running aground. Those ships that were firing on the huge German bunkers were key in punching holes in the German lines and getting our guys off the beach and inland. The captains of these ships should be considered heroes for risking their crews and ships in supporting the soldiers on the beach. The history of Omaha would have been much different if it wasn't for their bravery. Their efforts were the turning point of the Americans' ultimate success at Omaha.

One of the three huge ships in front of the Vierville Draw was the USS *McCook*, which was targeting pillboxes, bunkers, buildings, and machine gun nests. As we stood watching from the deck of our LCT, we saw the *McCook* fire directly into the bunker that was firing its 88 out to sea on an angle. The *McCook* had silenced one of the deadliest guns on Omaha. All the men on our deck started cheering as the echoes of the explosion thundered through the sky above the ocean. We started shaking hands as we watched smoke bellowing out of the bunker's gun port. You can't imagine how good it felt seeing that devastating bunker go up in a blaze.

We were unable to load or unload vehicles from other cargo ships without a front ramp. That, along with a buckled hull and being partially flooded, essentially put us out of commission, so we spent the rest of our day picking men out of the water.

In the afternoon, the only thing we could do was float around in the water and helplessly watch men and equipment pouring onto the beach. Finally, the word came late in the afternoon that the beach had been taken and the Americans were moving inland.

At the end of our day, we beached our LCT a third time. As we slid our LCT onto the beach that final time, we further damaged the hull that had been crippled during our second landing.

From our third landing location, the beach looked like a parking lot of burnt-out vehicles and tanks. Men were lying dead everywhere. The Seabees were directing bulldozers as they coldly and methodically pushed bodies into piles to quickly make room for the landing of more trucks, tanks, Jeeps, and supplies. At the same time, thousands of men were landing up and down the beach. We watched as these men landed and were quickly organized into groups to be moved inland before nightfall on the one paved road in Vierville.

As the sun was going down, we stood on the deck of our landing craft and watched in amazement how huge the operation was. Out at sea, hundreds of ships were moving toward shore as they were getting ready to unload. Large troop ships pulled up to the beach and dropped hundreds of men directly onto land.

As I stood on the deck, I thought back to standing on this very same deck earlier that morning watching the bombardment of the shore knocking the hell out of the enemies' defenses. At that time, I was sure the bombardment would make our landing pretty easy. We all watched that bombardment, and we had *all* been sure that no object, structure, or person could survive. We had no idea how wrong we were and what was still in store for us.

That evening we found out our flotilla, the Gunfire Support Group, had lost 75 percent of our landing craft. Hearing that, I could hardly believe we had survived. When we had hit the beach that morning, I was sure it was the last day of my life. I could hardly believe I lived through it. When we couldn't retract, I thought all of us would die and our ship would be lost.

"Now, fifty-four years later, I'm still amazed I came through that day without a scratch, and I still can't believe we didn't lose a crew member. The worst physical thing that happened to me on that day was that I had gotten chafed raw from wet clothes and salt water. I guess I made out better than Tillins, who had some very black and blue and swollen arms—which, by the way, he said he was thankful for. As he put it, "I would rather be black and blue than dead."

We were all changed emotionally and mentally after that day. After seeing the things we had seen, we would never be the same men again. Most of us held ourselves together and focused on our duty, knowing we were doing a tough job that had to be done. There were other men who weren't doing so well; some were even crying they were so emotionally upset."

-Bill Grannetino, 1998

After being awake for almost twenty-four hours, I was completely exhausted. I finally lay down on a half-burnt mattress and went to sleep. Being so physically depleted, I slept through whatever sounds of war rang out during the first night on Omaha.

[CHAPTER 4]

The Days After D-Day

I WOKE UP THE NEXT MORNING before the sun had peeked over the horizon. The motorized sounds of large equipment and all kinds of moving vehicles echoed along the beach. Thousands of men were being deployed and hundreds of ships were out in the ocean waiting to unload their cargo. Huge Landing Craft called LSTs (Landing Ships Tanks) were on the beach unloading tanks, trucks, Jeeps, supplies, and all the materials of war.

Medical personnel were loading the wounded onto LCTs and taking them to ships offshore for transport back to England. At the same time, other LCTs were unloading men and cargo from other ships offshore and bringing their loads to many different distribution points.

Barbed wire that had been part of the German defenses had been collected and placed in large circles. These enclosures created makeshift holding pens for German prisoners. They were held like this until they could be shipped to England.

Even with the enemy pushed back, there was still plenty of danger all around us. Navy demolition crews were disarming the mines tied to the beach obstacles. When the obstacles were safe, bulldozers would knock them down and push them along with the other obstacles into piles that were out of the way of the unloading operation. Other crews of soldiers were clearing mines that had been buried in the ground above the beach.

The Seabees were towing vehicles and tanks that had been blown up during the fighting into an orderly parking lot fashion, creating a makeshift junkyard. There were trucks being followed by groups of men picking up debris and twisted steel from the beach. Cleared areas were becoming lay-down areas for boxes and crates filled with supplies. Everything from food to weapons was being stocked in these areas. Trucks were already being loaded at these supply areas to be driven inland for our frontline troops. It appeared to me that one of the most important items being moved on that first morning after D-Day was gasoline. Fuel was needed for our supply trucks so they could keep moving supplies forward and for our tanks fighting on the front lines.

Tents that served as makeshift command centers had been set up on the beach. The officers assembled in these quarters were organizing all the activities. One of our crew members said Corky was up there getting our orders as we spoke. While we waited for Corky, we ate cold leftovers from our pre-D-Day dinner. When Corky returned with our orders, he said we would be used as general laborers on the beach, because our LCT was out of commission. He told me I would take charge of our seamen for these work duties. Then he informed us that our first duty assignment would be taking care of the American dead. No one was looking forward to that gruesome duty. It was later after the war that I learned some two thousand Americans died at Omaha on that first day.

We were directed by some Seabees to piles of dead soldiers that had been pushed into heaps by bulldozers clearing the beach for oncoming men and equipment from the night before. These piles of bodies stood as a gruesome shrine to the horrific events of the previous day. The bodies were a dreadful sight to behold. They were twisted and ripped, many had missing limbs, some had been torn to pieces, and several had been horribly burned. The sand at the base of the pile of dead was completely saturated with blood. The bloody bodies were filthy with dirt and sand and had countless open wounds. I believe Satan himself would have turned away in disgust.

Our job was to lay the bodies in rows. When the bodies were laid out, we were to remove all of their military equipment—everything from backpacks and handguns to grenades and ammunition belts. Then we had to remove all their personal belongings from their pockets and lay those items on their chests.

We all stood in silence, almost afraid to touch a dead body. Finally Tillins said, "Let's be men about this," and he stepped up, grabbed the feet of one of the fallen soldiers, and pulled the body out onto the ground. I grabbed the hands and we laid this guy out and started to gingerly remove his gear and empty his pockets. Following our lead, the rest of the crew started removing bodies from the pile and making rows of the dead.

Later on, another group of soldiers from the Quartermasters Graves Registration Service collected the dead and their personal belongings, filled out paper tags, and then tied those tags to the bodies. They then loaded the bodies onto trucks and transported them to temporary burial sites. Their personal effects and records were taken to a makeshift temporary Quartermasters headquarters that had been set up on the beach during the night.

We had been on this horrible duty for hours when suddenly we were attacked by two German planes that swooped down on the beach and strafed it with gunfire. Everybody ran for cover, getting behind or under anything that could be found. As quickly as they came in, they were gone. One quick pass is all they made. I don't think anyone was hit or killed—at least not in our area of beach. Some equipment and supplies were hit and now had bullet holes in them. We waited a bit and watched to see if the coast was clear before going back to work. There wasn't any official notice of all clear given. Somehow it was just assumed.

When we were done laying out the dead from the bulldozed piles of bodies, we were given litters and sent up the beach and inland to pick up any remaining bodies that had not yet been collected. When we got up to and beyond the sea wall toward the top of the beach, I saw enormous areas of sand made red by spilt blood. The memory of it still shakes me; it was an indelible impression. In some sections, you couldn't walk in the sand without stepping in dried blood. Beyond the seawall in the more inland section of beach the dead were lying in minefields. These areas were surrounded with signs saying "MINEFIELD" and cordoned off with rope. Here combat engineering soldiers were clearing the mine areas. As they cleared these areas, they also took care of the dead.

The whole area we were working in was covered with craters from our naval bombardment. Along with those craters were the craters from the Germans' artillery and mortar fire. Strangely, we didn't see any indication of the air corps bombardment. Just beyond this area, we came across German trenches and foxholes that had been dug at the top of these hills. Behind those we found some deep concrete pits the Germans had built. These pit-type bunkers still had German mortars and their rounds stocked in them. We could see that it was from there that the German mortar crews were firing at us. It was apparent that these mortar crews worked with a very limited view of the beach and had to have a spotter give them direction as they fired.

Looking out toward the ocean from this vantage point, we could see other crews of sailors in small boats just off the shore fishing the dead out of the sea. They were using small winches mounted on the side of their boats to retrieve these men. Most of the dead soldiers had flotation belts around their waists and were floating in the water; many with heavy packs were floating head down, feet up. The sailors in the boats would loop a rope around one leg and lift the dead soldiers upside-down into their boats. Still other crews on the beach were taking bodies out of tanks and trucks, "tagging and bagging" them as well.

Working our way up the hillsides beyond the German foxholes and closer to the backside of the huge concrete bunkers, we started to come across dead Germans as well. These bodies were not laid out; they were just unceremoniously loaded onto trucks and hauled away. I have no idea where they were taken, nor did any of us really care. Right or wrong, the sight of seeing dead German soldiers after experiencing the events of yesterday provided all of us with a sense of fulfilled vengeance.

As we worked beyond those German bunkers, we saw that some American soldiers were confronting a French woman who had been collaborating with the German soldiers. At first she was arguing, then she was screaming and fighting with them as they tried to restrain her. They were hollering back at her, calling her a "pig" and a "slut." She tried to kick them and was spitting on them. Two of the soldiers grabbed her by the hair and dragged her to a tree. They slapped her in the face and knocked her to the ground. Then they grabbed her and ripped at her clothes, stripping her naked. They tied her to the tree. She was fighting and yelling the whole time. One of the soldiers pulled his knife and held it to her neck. She was still yelling, spitting, and fighting. The soldier holding the knife yelled back at her. "If you want to sleep with the Germans, you may as well sleep with the dead ones too." With that, the soldier stuck his knife between her legs and pulled it to her chest, dumping her insides out on the ground.

I had seen more than my fair share of death and dying over the last twenty-four hours. Way too much. Up until that point, I had managed to keep control of my emotions, but with the sight of that French woman being disemboweled, I trembled with emotions that are almost impossible to describe. It was a combination of complete disgust, hatred, intense anger, and some sort of overall military embarrassment and shame. It bothered me so intensely that I felt physically ill. Without a doubt, the sight of that one murdered woman seemed a worse fate than all the dead bodies we were picking up off the beach. I looked away, wondering to myself, *Just who are we? Are we this awful?* This was depraved murder, and it was distinctly different from what had happened yesterday to thousands of men on both sides. We looked at each other, wondering what we should do. Some said it should be reported. Others said they didn't see a thing. I didn't know what to think, nor did I know whose job it was to deal with something like this. The one thing I did know was what *my* job was, so I decided to do my job. I went back to work picking up bodies and so did the rest of our guys.

Later on, we were told the soldier who killed that woman was from a division that had lost all but two of their men in the first wave to hit the shore the morning before. They said she told this survivor how glad she was so many Americans died in the invasion. Then she warned him that it wouldn't be long until the Germans launched their counterattack and threw the Americans back into the sea. She threatened that, after the counterattack, there would be a lot more Americans dead just like his dead friends. She said she would be glad to see it. She retaliated by saying that the Americans would then be the "pigs" and "sluts." For some, this justified her death and its means. Most of us knew it was wrong and no story could justify it. I don't know who cut her down or what happened to her body, but we never heard another word about it.

We continued working, picking up the dead until early evening, and then returned to our LCT for the night. We were all physically exhausted, hungry, and tired. We had hot food and then sacked out to get some sleep.

During the night, we woke up when the Germans launched an air attack on the navy's ships just off the shoreline. I knew that despite our exhaustion, there would be "no rest for the weary." The air attack was happening pretty far to our east; we could hear the commotion as we ran out on deck to see what was going on. One of our seamen on our LCT who had been standing watch during the night said a couple of German planes flew over, dropping yellow flares over the ships anchored off the shore. When the sky lit up, another wave of German fighters flew in, attacking illuminated ships. He said that tracers were like shooting stars streaking across the sky, some coming from the ships and others from the enemy planes. The entire event only lasted a few minutes and was over very quickly. When things were quiet for a while, we all went back to sleep.

Later that same night, we were up again and back out on deck when some inland German artillery opened fire on the ships anchored off the coast. Now that it was dark, the Germans' artillery was protected from any accurate counterfire coming back from our navy ships. Knowing that, they attempted firing a few rounds of artillery at the U.S. fleet. This shelling also happened to our east, as it was targeted more toward the center of Omaha Beach. As far as we could tell, the entire attack consisted of only six or seven rounds of artillery fire. The next day we were told that several of the ships in the targeted area had evacuated their crews, not knowing how limited the attack would be. No ships had been hit.

Even after those disturbances during the night, we were all up before the crack of dawn on our third morning at Vierville. It was another damp morning in the mid-fifties as we waited to receive our orders for the upcoming day. The beach was even busier than the day before as thousands of soldiers continued to pour into Normandy. There were now even more trucks, tanks, and supplies being unloaded from ships and landing craft of all sizes. There were officers from Command coordinating the supplies being delivered, and then other officers organizing sending them to the front. These same officers were now being set up in command centers that originated in the captured German bunkers.

As we were waiting for our orders of the day, we knew there were still many dead bodies to be collected further inland and in some of the rougher-terrain areas. When Corky returned from command, he let us know that we wouldn't be collecting dead bodies today, which prompted an immediate rush of relief through every man in our crew. We all felt like we had done our duty for the Quartermasters Graves Registration Service and that we had tended to more than our fair share of fallen soldiers. Corky then told us we would be helping with the building of a floating harbor.

We were put to work helping the Seabees hook up steel decks that were supported by huge floating pontoons. At the end of these piers were huge concrete boxes called Mulberrys. They had been built in England and had recently arrived after being towed by tugs across the English Channel. When they arrived at Omaha, the tugs pushed these floating concrete boxes toward the place where they were then sunk, creating a concrete structure as the end for the floating decks. In all, there was more than a mile of different flexible steel roadways extending out to sea. The long length of these floating roadways made handling the twenty-five-foot difference of high to low tide much more tolerable. When the tide was in, the complete system was floating. When the tide was out, about a third of the roadways were sitting on sand. As we worked, the constant movement of waves coming into shore tossed us and the floating pontoons back and forth, making our work much more difficult. Even though the long lengths of steel roadways were tied down to the sea floor and attached to the concrete Mulberrys, they were still being pushed around by the powerful waves, making them somewhat unstable for vehicle traffic. To solve that problem, the Seabees decided to create a breakwater to stop the motion of the waves from moving the roadways around.

After working for two or three days with the Seabees on those floating steel harbors, we were reassigned to another Seabee crew to create the much-needed breakwaters. The Seabees explained that because the seas were so rough, we would need to create a breakwater by sinking a row of Liberty ships in shallow water to block the incoming ocean. This would stop the waves from continually banging against the floating steel roads of the harbor. They told us that their plan was to rig the bottom of these empty ships with explosives. Then when the ships were towed to their place in the breakwater's row, the explosives would be detonated.

I told the Seabees with whom I was working that I could sink the ships without using explosives to blow out the bottoms of the ships. I explained that I had a full understanding of how water flowed in and out of the ship. For the different water functions such as cooling, firefighting, sewage discharge, and using the distillers to make fresh water, the flow of water would vary predictably. I told them that I had worked in the shipyards and had seen and worked on the inner workings of all those systems inside the hulls of ships. The Seabees passed this on to their superiors, who were very interested in knowing how to sink the ships without explosives, because later they could pump the water out of the ships and refloat them. Some Seabees felt it would take too long to flood the ships this way. I eased their concerns and told them it wasn't a problem, that I could flood the ships and sink them in a couple of hours. Having convinced them, I was assigned to lead a crew of Seabees in sinking the first few ships.

Tugs towed and pushed the Liberty ships into place. When they were in their places in the breakwater row, anchors were dropped and they were tied together end to end with cables and mooring ropes. Next, I led the work crews into the first few ships, showing and explaining to them the key valves they needed to turn to start flooding the ships. After we had begun the sinking of two or three of the ships, they had a pretty good idea of how to use the systems. We broke up into a few small crews and had all the ships taking on water within hours. The ships sank one after another, creating the breakwater and stopping the waves from pounding into the Mulberry Harbors and their steel decks.

Once the Seabees had completed assembling the harbors, large ships could anchor next to the piers and unload cargo that was driven directly to the beach on the steel decks floating on pontoons. Huge amounts of cargo started moving much more quickly inland to support our troops fighting on the front. After the harbors were up and running, we were reassigned to being cargo handlers. We helped on the beach in any way needed.

During the first few days we were on the beach, our area of Omaha was shelled by German artillery every night without exception—a constant reminder that our enemy beyond the beach was undeterred by their loss there. This artillery only fired a few shots each night with the purpose of keeping their locations uncompromised. Finally, about a week or more after

D-Day, the shelling from the Germans stopped as the American troops moved further inland. Each day that we were on the beach the big guns on our Iowa-class battleships would fire inland. We had no idea what their target was, but we knew that it meant the enemy was still close enough to be reached from the shore. Iowa-class battleships can accurately fire at targets up to twenty miles away.

When the Mulberry Harbor and the steel decks had been in place for a little over a week, a huge gale blew in off the Atlantic, devastating the coast. This storm was so furious, it created enormous waves that pounded the floating harbor system. All shipping and material handling completely stopped during this storm that went on for three or four days. Even though we had created breakwaters out of Liberty ships, and the Seabees had securely fastened the harbor to the seabed, the ocean was so turbulent that the harbor was being torn to pieces by the size of the waves created by this gale. Several of our LCTs, some small landing craft, and other small boats sank. Many more of the smaller craft were blown onto the shore and stranded on land. As the storm raged, the floating pontoons and steel decks were totally destroyed. The Allies had been unloading nearly a hundred ships during the course of a twenty-four-hour day onto our Mulberry Harbors. It became obvious that this storm was going to put our Omaha port out of commission permanently.

After the storm ended, we walked around looking at the damage caused by Mother Nature. It was unbelievable. Millions and millions of dollar's worth of equipment had been destroyed. Regardless of the gale and the devastation, the navy quickly reacted and abandoned the harbor. LCTs immediately took over again, moving supplies from the cargo ships to shore. Several crews were promptly put to work cleaning up the destroyed remains of the harbor.

In our sector of Omaha, we immediately started sinking more Liberty ships to create a larger system of breakwaters to aid the LCTs with landing supplies. I was still assigned to the crews working with the Seabees, once again helping their tugs towing and pushing more Liberty ships into place to be sunk. Just as before, when the ships were in place, they were moored together. Then the same crews went onto ship after ship and scuttled them. It took several days to get these larger breakwaters into place.

Once the additional Liberty ships had been sunk and our breakwaters were in place, I was ordered to rejoin several of our crews helping the Seabees with the cleanup operation of the destroyed Mulberry Harbors. This work went on for a week or so. When the harbor's components were cleared, the pieces that were in better shape were pulled aside to be shipped east to another fully operational British Mulberry Harbor. There they consolidated these parts to create one larger, complete functioning harbor.

Then we were reassigned to general work duties and material handling. In time, the ramp on our LCT was replaced and all the holes blown through the hull were repaired. Now with our ship in working order, a few fellows on our crew and I were operating LCT 9134(A), unloading ships, and hauling supplies to shore. This was a very busy time for us, as we spent long days hauling supplies and occasionally doing manual labor. Most of our duties from ship to shore were to bring tanks, halftracks, and trucks ashore. For the most part when doing manual labor, we helped with the loading of trucks that were part of the operation of moving supplies inland. It wasn't terribly exciting, but in this line of work, "boring" often meant "safe," which was a tradeoff we all welcomed.

After following this routine for several days, late one afternoon Corky called our crew together. He informed us that several of our crew were going to be reassigned. He let us know that a few fellows were going to stay with the LCT and continue unloading ships. The rest of us were going to join several American troops assisting the British Army. He told us that the British were supposed to have taken the city of Caen on D-Day, and that even after a couple of weeks of fighting and several attempts, they still hadn't pushed the Germans out of Caen. Our American commanders had decided to help the British with some reinforcements. They were now gathering any available men and sending them to help those British troops. Because most of us were doing nothing more than busy work, it was decided that half our crew would be assigned to this new duty. He read a list of names and it included both Tillins and me. So much for boring and safe.

The next morning, several of our crew along with Tillins and myself gathered our personal belongings and reported to an army supply tent. There we were issued army clothing, a loaded backpack, a rifle, and ammunition. Next we were loaded onto trucks and driven to a British camp north of Caen.

[CHAPTER 5]

The Battle for Caen

WE ARRIVED AT THE BRITISH camp midday, at which point all of us Americans were paired up and assigned to British squads. Understanding the value of having a friend in unfamiliar territory, Tillins and I gladly paired up and were assigned to a group of eight British soldiers. These British guys seemed like a bunch of really nice fellows with great attitudes, which was remarkable considering they had spent the last two weeks trying to fight their way into Caen.

As we introduced ourselves, the looks of confusion were clearly visible on their faces, and their first question to us was, Why in the hell were a couple of American navy guys assigned to a British infantry squad? We told them we really didn't have any idea why and that their guess was as good as ours. All we knew was that we were a couple of sailors following orders.

The British fellows told us that their group was serving under General Montgomery and that we would soon be making another attempt at liberating Caen, a city setting inland from the coast about twelve miles. They went on to say it was originally planned that Caen would be liberated on D-Day. Unfortunately for the British, the Germans were heavily fortified and well reinforced from D-Day to that present time. They explained that there had been three previous attempts to overtake the Germans defending Caen and that each attempt had ended in failure. Regardless, they seemed optimistic that with any luck, this fourth attempt would be the one to finally take the city back.

We were posted on the north side of Caen in a section controlled by the British that was considered safe. Tillins and I were given our first duty, which was to dig trenches. The British soldiers in our squad weren't too happy about having to dig trenches. They felt it was just busy work and that the trenches would never really be needed, because in a day or so we would be moving forward into Caen. The way Tillins and I saw it, digging those trenches was preferable to confronting the Germans on the front lines. After hours of digging, the trenches were finished.

The British officers had us gather planks and wood from nearby war-torn houses, barns, and other buildings. The wood we gathered would cover the top of the trenches with structures that functioned as flat roofs. The flat roofs were built propped up on the south side so soldiers on the inside could shoot out of the trenches toward the enemy south of us. The British officers said that hundreds of lives had been lost through poorly constructed trenches. The shelling they had experienced earlier apparently had been so severe, it had killed many of their troops, although the trenches had been dug very well. It was then decided that when it was possible, trenches would be covered over with wood. These roofs were constructed in a way that would not interfere with a good view for shooting at the enemy.

That evening, we took our place in the trenches. As we sat quietly with our boots sinking into the moist soil, each man primed his grenades and loaded his weapon in preparation of an enemy attack during the night. The British soldiers in our squad told us that the British soldiers on the frontlines were having a hell of a time with the Germans. They expected that tomorrow we would be joining those hard-pressed troops and would as well be on the British frontlines.

During our first night with the British, we saw several hundred Allied planes fly overhead and then heard bombing toward the city south of us. It was like the thunder of an approaching storm rolling in from the distance. After the air attack ended, we heard what sounded like several hundred more thunderclaps as pieces of artillery began firing into the city. At about the same time the artillery started, naval battleships some twenty miles away began firing their huge guns over our heads, adding to the bombardment of Caen. Thousands of tons of ordnances fell relentlessly on Caen during our first night with the British. For hours, Caen looked like a fireworks show filled with explosions and burning fires. Tillins and I sat with the British, and we all agreed that next to nothing could live through that devastation. Then I remembered that we had wrongly assumed that same thing before our landing at Omaha.

At first light we got out of our trenches. Our boots were muddy and damp from the moist ground in the bottom of the trenches. The British were making a fire to heat water for morning tea, which was part of their typical morning routine. Then out of nowhere came the screeching sound of incoming mortar fire from the Germans. There were one, two, then three explosions in the first few seconds of the attack. The British quickly abandoned their tea as we all rushed back to our trenches for cover and prepared to endure this attack. The British soldiers now fully realized the value of the roofs we had built over the trenches. We all agreed it was amazing that the Germans were this close, and we wondered where they came from and how many of them were there. If they came out of Caen, how had they survived the bombardment last night and how long had they been out there watching us? Would they be attacking us with infantry after this bombardment? We just didn't know, and that uncertainty was what scared us the most.

Looking up and down the line of men hunkered down in the trenches, I could see nothing but pale white complexions. It was clear that all of us soldiers were equally afraid of the incoming mortar barrage. To make it even worse, the Germans opened up with small artillery fire. I kept trying to reassure myself that as long as we were down in our trenches, we were going to be okay. Tillins was shaking like a leaf. He could not say a word.

Finally, after an hour of shelling, there was silence. The only sounds we could hear were the moans and groans of a couple of British guys wounded by shrapnel. The medics immediately went to their aid. Only one shell landed directly on top of one of the trenches, killing two British soldiers under the wooden covers. We figured that it wouldn't be long until we would be attacked by several tanks, followed by infantry. As we waited to see what would happen, the British fellows gathered wood and made another fire, this time down in the trenches, as they heated their morning tea. Apparently not even the threat of death could stop British soldiers from having their tea! Fortunately, to our surprise, the attack never came.

After we sat and waited for a while, our British sergeant told us to get ready because he'd just been informed that we would shortly be heading for Caen. During the time we were getting ready, several British tanks had been brought up from the rear. The plan was that they would take the lead as we made our way into Caen. Everybody felt a little better knowing tanks would be escorting us. We weren't sure where the German mortar crews were at this time, but we were sure they wouldn't open up on us again now that we had a couple of tanks. We also hoped that when we reached the edge of the city and then made our way completely inside, we would be out of harm's way. We hoped that anyone inside the city after last night's bombing and the fires that had followed would already be dead.

While we were following the tanks on the roads just outside the city, the stench of rotten carcasses swept over us, followed by the sight of several dead farm animals. It wasn't long until we were passing dead soldiers, first the British and then the Germans. Tanks, trucks, Jeeps, and half-tracks were sitting blown up and burnt out everywhere. I remember thinking to myself, *If I had the tools, I could salvage enough different parts from all the destroyed tanks to build several functional ones.* Nearly every building we passed on the way into Caen had burned, was bombed out, or was completely destroyed. The bombing the night before had left Caen looking less like a city and more like a burning pile of rubble.

When we finally got into Caen, I could not believe that the destruction there was even worse. Hardly a building was standing. The devastation was so bad, it was difficult to discern where the city roads were. Later we would see Le Harve, which was as heavily damaged as Caen, but we felt sure these were the two most devastated cities we would ever see in France. I wondered where the people were who lived there. Surely there were survivors hiding somewhere in all of the desolation. It was hard to imagine how many bodies of French civilians were mixed in all that rubble. God, it was awful. I couldn't help but wonder how we could justify killing that many innocent people in order to kill the enemy.

Now that we had arrived at the city, we met up with several other squads of British. The officers in charge planned to join the squads together and start clearing Germans out of the city, street by street. The first thing we were ordered to do was dig foxholes for the night. Our British sergeant wanted us taking cover as quickly as possible so we wouldn't be taking the time to cover the top of the trenches with lumber. Tillins and I dug a hole inside a collapsed building. This would give us extra cover behind the fallen stone walls. We ate and slept in these holes for the night. In the morning we gathered in preparation for our advance deeper into the city.

Our squad would be advancing without any tanks because the roads were totally filled with debris from collapsed buildings. Our tanks were sent to a less devastated section of the city to help clear those sections while we worked our way through all the collapsed buildings. It was previously planned that we would meet up with our tanks and our trucks on the other side of northern Caen before entering southern Caen.

Tillins and I advanced with a group of British foot soldiers on a main road in our squad's section of Caen. We moved in and out of the various buildings, using them as cover until we came to a large factory comprised of several large buildings. When we started crossing the loading yard in the center of the plant, enemy fire opened up. Several men who were leading the squad fell dead. The rest of us took cover and started returning fire.

From somewhere on the opposite end of the factory, the Germans had a machine gun set up. Several other German soldiers were shooting from doors or windows, while others had taken positions on the different roofs of the factory's buildings.

Within the first few minutes of shooting, several more British soldiers were dead. The fighting was very confusing. The smallest movement drew enemy fire. We couldn't see the enemy anywhere; they were well hidden. Our British sergeant starting yelling out orders, ordering us to fall back. Tillins and I ran back through the inside of the factory's shipping building.

When we got back to the main road, we were quickly divided up and sent to positions to defend ourselves. Tillins and I were sent with several others of the remaining British soldiers to stop any flanking attempt by the Germans. No sooner were we set up when they began trying to flank our position. As we watched their advance, we were told to hold our fire until the last possible moment.

When we could see about ten or twelve of the Germans within what I would say was about thirty-five to forty yards of us, we opened fire. Several fell dead; others ran for cover into the collapsed buildings. We shot at them and they returned fire for a few minutes. Then, all of a sudden, the firefight stopped and it became quiet. They were now holding fire and we held fire. Seeing no enemy to shoot at, we just maintained our positions. Both sides were on watch for each other's next move. With this break in the fighting, our sergeant called for reinforcements.

As we waited for our reinforcements, we also continued watching for the Germans' next move. We kept particularly careful watch on the areas where we last saw the enemy. As I was peeking over the collapsed stone wall, I could smell the smoke of wood burning. I turned to see what was burning and saw British soldiers starting a fire to heat water for tea. I couldn't believe it. At any minute we could be overrun and killed! There were men not too far from us lying dead—men that we had just killed. How could they be thinking of tea at a time like this? How could they not stay on watch in the event the Germans made a move? I just looked at Tillins and shook my head. Tillins said under his breath, "It must be some really good tea."

When our reinforcements showed up, they had an American bazooka with them. I watched as our British sergeant and these guys talked about the best way to attack the building where the Germans were taking cover. It was decided that we would all get into different angled positions so we could put different angles of fire on the building. In the center of this, the bazooka team would start off by firing into the front window of the building where the Germans were last seen. Then, immediately, we infantry soldiers would start shooting to keep pressure on them as the bazooka reloaded to fire again. The overall plan was to attack and keep attacking until they were all dead, had retreated, or had surrendered—whichever came first.

It only took a few minutes until we were all in position. The bazooka team got ready to fire by first looking left and then right. With that, they fired and there was a huge explosion. Fire blew out all the doors and windows. Immediately we added fire while the bazooka was reloading. Wood splintered and stone collapsed and fell. The bazooka fired several more shots into several other main areas as we continued shooting and keeping the pressure on with more and more continuous fire.

Then we were all ordered to hold our fire. I figured we had gotten all of them; I was sure that nothing or no one could live through what we had just witnessed. Within a few seconds of holding our fire, we started receiving fire from within the buildings our bazooka had just decimated. I couldn't believe it! How could they still be alive? If they had lived through that, they should have been waving a white flag in surrender, not shooting back. Those sons-of-bitches were some really tough bastards; they had to have been the bravest men I had ever seen—or the dumbest. They had to know they were going to die if they didn't give up, but instead they were shooting back.

Within a few seconds we were all shooting again as the bazooka fired into the center of what was left of the occupied building. Several Germans were killed in that blast. Their shooting stopped for a moment. I expected the final survivors to start filing out with their hands over their heads. To our continued surprise, the few who were left started shooting again. It looked as though we would have to kill every single one of those bastards. With that, we kept heavy fire on them while the bazooka fired into several main doors and windows of the buildings from which they were firing. Finally, all their shooting stopped, indicating the men inside were finally dead. The pile of debris that was once a building was now burning, and heavy smoke was pouring out of openings that were once doors and windows.

We walked over toward the buildings and looked at the dead Germans. I couldn't believe it. Not one of those guys looked to be over eighteen or twenty years old. They were nothing more than kids. We couldn't understand why they didn't surrender. One of the older British soldiers said, "It's like flushing rats out of a garbage can. If they had any good sense, they would have given up and lived." I just kept thinking to myself that they were some of the toughest and bravest guys I had ever seen in my life. I still couldn't believe how they fought back as we were firing a bazooka on their position. They had to know they were all going to die for nothing.

Our engagement wasn't over yet. We had a break for a few minutes before we made our way to the next street, where we engaged the enemy again in a similar fight. Three times that day we were fully engaged in fighting street to street. In the last fight, we held one end of a school and the Germans held the other. Our fighting was inside and outside of the building and on different floors all at the same time. I hadn't been so scared since D-Day.

Several of the British died in that fight. After intense fighting, we finally overtook the whole school, killing every one of the Germans. They were again fighting to the death rather than choosing to retreat or surrender.

The close-quarters fighting continued for several days. Time and time again we had to dig those tough Germans out of the buildings where they had taken refuge. Most times they would fight to the death, but as the battle continued, they started to lose their spirit and surrender rather than die for nothing. Many of the British fighting with us had died. The cost of liberating northern Caen couldn't be measured in currency. More accurately, it had to be counted in blood and in the lives lost on both sides of the battlefield. It was truly awful.

We didn't get much sleep during this time and had little time to eat. By the end of the first week, the street-to-street fighting in northern Caen had eased up. Hungry as we were, we became pretty good at scavenging. Somebody found several dozen eggs and loaves of white bread that had most likely belonged to the Germans. By our standards, it was a meal fit for a king. The British started a fire and began heating water to make their tea. Tillins and I cut-off the flat top of a fifty-gallon barrel and placed it over a fire like a makeshift griddle. Then Tillins used it to make scrambled eggs. One of the Brits found some beer and brought it to our makeshift meal. After days of nerve-wracking fighting, we were glad to sit back for a moment and relax, eating eggs with bread and drinking beer. For that brief moment, we were blessedly oblivious to the travesties we had witnessed during the last few weeks.

Bulldozers began clearing the streets of northern Caen so that tanks could get through and reassemble for the next push. Truckloads of supplies could then also be brought to the front to re-arm and re-equip our troops. When we had finally taken and secured northern Caen, we began our preparations to drive the Germans out of southern Caen.

With an opportune, albeit short, break in the action before we headed into southern Caen, we got some much-needed sleep. Several of us washed up and shaved. We even washed our clothing the best we could. Tillins and I took a walk through the area we had just been fighting in. We saw the British engineers moving through the numerous ruins of Caen looking for mines and booby-traps. While we were on our little expedition, I found a machine gun on a dead Brit that I took for myself. Surely it would benefit me more than it would him. It felt good that from now on I would be fighting with a machine gun instead of a rifle.

While walking around, Tillins and I came across a British soldier "examining" one dead German after another. He was holding some sort of device in his hand. When he was bent over one of the dead, we could see that he had a pair of pliers in his hand. We watched this guy roll the dead Germans over and pry open their mouths, which were stiff from rigor mortis. As he knelt over the dead bodies, he would first push on their chin with one hand while holding down on their forehead with the other. When he got the mouth open a little, he would put both hands between their teeth and pry their jaws open as far as he could. Then he held their mouths open with one hand on their chin and grabbed them by the hair with the other hand. After doing that, he would roll and twist their heads into a position that allowed sunlight to shine into their mouths. As he did this, he was talking to them. He would say, "Okay, let's roll over. Come on, fellow; let me see what you got. Open up now. What do you have in there for me?" When he had good light shining into the dead man's mouth, his head would start bobbing and weaving around to get a good look at his upper and lower teeth. Then we could hear him say, "Ah, there we go. Look at that … that's what we're looking for." With that, he would pull out his pliers, put it into their mouth, and start pulling. Next thing you know, he dropped the dead man's head and lifted the pliers up holding a tooth. He would stand up as he was turning and rolling the pliers, examining a tooth.

Eventually he saw us watching him. He looked at us for a moment and said, "There's plenty of gold here for everybody. Almost every one of these German bastards has one or two gold fillings in his mouth. Come on and get some, and you can go home a rich man after this war is over." After he said this, he held his pliers up and again examined all sides of the tooth he'd just pulled. "There's a good one," he said. With that, he took a cloth bag out of his pocket and dropped the tooth into this bag, which looked like it was almost full.

Tillins spoke for both of us when he said, "No thanks, that's not for us."

"No," I said, "it's not in my category."

"Well," he said, "that's your loss, not mine." With that he looked to the next group of dead Germans and headed toward them. Tillins looked at me and said, "Sick bastard." With that we headed back to our squad.

During this short break in the action, we were regrouped and the officers reorganized our squads. Several of the British squads were joined together with Canadian squads who were operating just to our west. I think I had to explain to the Canadians at least fifty times why a couple of American navy guys were fighting with the British infantry in Caen.

In preparation for our next move, we rejoined the tanks. They would be taking the lead as we made our next push. That push would be in cooperation with the Canadians, so that we were simultaneously moving across all the remaining bridges that led into southern Caen. Our tanks, along with the Canadians' tanks, would hit all the bridges at once in overwhelming numbers and drive the Germans back before they could destroy the bridges.

As the troops got ready, Tillins and I were directed to help with the refueling of the tanks, trucks, and other vehicles. We also assisted with the re-arming of the tanks and the artillery crews. While we were doing this, several British squads of soldiers passed us riding bicycles. I didn't know where they came from or where they were going. Tillins stood there just shaking his head, and then he looked at me with wide eyes. He said, "Boy, these British are strange fellows. Who the hell goes to war riding a bicycle?"

When evening came, the French civilians started to enter the streets, thanking both British and Canadian soldiers for liberating them from the Germans. Many had bottles of wine and were offering the soldiers drinks. The women were kissing soldiers and saying thank you. A few were carrying French flags and hanging them up to display. You could tell that they were thrilled to be free of the German oppression. We were all feeling pretty special as large convoys of trucks showed up with food and medical supplies for the French citizens. I'll never forget how they were smiling and drinking from their wine bottles, all the while they were yelling in French, "Liberation, liberation, liberation!"

After working all day and half the night, we were spread out by the officers evenly behind several tank brigades preparing to attack southern Caen. We were in position and ready to follow the tanks scheduled to attack just before first light. Officers came around to each squad and briefed them about what they should expect beyond the bridges leading into southern Caen and then gave us our specific assignments. At the end of our briefing, the officers told us that we would be attacking after an air bombardment that would be taking place in the early morning, just before first light.

During the night, we took cover a far distance back from the bridges. We sat on the rubble of several bombed-out buildings—just a sample of what we would find as we entered southern Caen. We were all extremely tense as we waited for the command to attack. Tillins looked at me for a few moments then smiled and said in a low voice as he put that dead pan look on his face, "You know, Bill, a fellow could get killed around here." We both laughed a little, despite the unknown events that awaited us.

Several British soldiers joined us as new reinforcements who were assigned to our squad. For the umpteenth time, Tillins and I again found ourselves explaining how two American navy guys had been sent to help reinforce British troops as they were fighting their way into Caen. I can still hear the reaction of these new British reinforcements when they found out who we were and why we were there. I think we must have had heard it again at least twenty times that night: "American navy guys? What in the hell are you doing here?"

As we were waiting for first light, I checked my new weapon. The machine gun I had picked up earlier was a 303 Lewis automatic. I had put a full clip of 303 bullets on top of the gun and had three full clips hanging from my waist. The barrel was clean and all the moving parts were lubed and ready to go. I thought to myself, *I sure hope it serves me better than it did its previous guy*. We were ready and, like all the rest of the squads, just waiting for the orders to go.

Suddenly we heard planes coming, indicating the assault on our enemy was underway. It was the first wave of bombers starting the attack on southern Caen. Within minutes, we could hear them dropping tons of bombs south of us. Shortly after that bombardment, the British artillery commenced a second bombardment. Still later, there were two more waves of bombers that arrived over southern Caen, where they dropped their payloads.

After those bombardments, our ground operation got underway. Our squads were led by tanks that moved through gaps cleared earlier by demolition crews in the German minefields. Those minefields had been placed specifically to stop our access to the bridges that divided Caen's north from south. We were ordered to immediately follow in the tanks' tracks through these minefields and not to move left or right to avoid unintentionally veering out of the cleared lanes. As infantry, our job would be to engage the enemy—we expected to be holed up in the bombed-out buildings across the river.

When we got to the bridges, our tanks immediately started firing at targets. At first we infantry guys had little resistance. We assumed the German defenders were dead or still shaken by the air raids and the artillery barrage. *Well, that didn't last too long*, I thought to myself. The Germans opened up with their machine gun fire, killing several of our men. That slowed down our advance. We ran for cover as the German infantry now also opened up with their small arms. Our sergeant hollered, "Rifles, move up … advance, advance!" We advanced under German fire to the piles of debris that had been stacked up in front of the bridge entrance by the enemy to prevent our tanks from accessing the bridge. We started firing at the German soldiers on the other side of the river, as they were running for better positions.

Men were falling on both sides. This was the first time I shot my Lewis automatic. I fired into groups of attacking German soldiers and saw men fall, but because the firing from everybody else was so intense, I could not tell if I was hitting any of them or not. All I knew was I was shooting and men were falling.

As quickly as it had all started, it ended when the Germans made a hasty retreat because our tanks were pushing through the debris at the entrance of the bridge and crossing into southern Caen. We followed the tanks and took cover as soon as we got to the other side. When the tanks had advanced a half a mile or so into southern Caen, one of them suddenly exploded. It had been hit by a German anti-tank weapon. Then all hell broke loose. Mortars landed all around us, and artillery fire started coming in from far-off enemy artillery batteries.

That's when I heard a familiar sound—a sound that sent chills down my spine. It was the God-awful shrill sound of a German 88 firing. I remembered that terrible sound from the goddamn 88s that had fired on the beaches at Omaha. I could tell from the screaming shrill sound that these

88s were firing from the ridge far to our south. Tillins just shook his head as he listened to the screaming sound of death. With all this firepower now being directed at us, the Germans were turning the tide of this battle in their favor very quickly. They had dug several tanks into defensive positions that were heavily camouflaged and now were successfully targeting our lead tanks. This was really bad and getting worse by the minute.

We understood why the German troops had retreated so quickly. It was so those bastards could suck us in and then start to shell our position. They could then take out our tanks without having to worry about hitting their own troops. That German shelling completely stopped our advance. The officers ordered the infantry to start digging in. You had better believe that men were digging foxholes in just minutes. Tillins and I did not take the time to dig a foxhole; we were lying down in some sort of a stone basement entrance, taking cover from the explosions.

The artillery shelling stopped as the encounter had quickly turned into a tank battle. The Germans were now counterattacking by sending in their Panzer tanks. Even though our British tanks outnumbered the German Panzers, the Panzers were larger, tougher, and had bigger guns. As the German tanks began their assault, the German troops had another advantage. They were fighting from the higher ground, making it easier for them to see the battle develop and target our tanks below them. The British attack had been a major mistake, and it quickly turned into what looked sure to be a British disaster.

British tanks were being targeted and were exploding everywhere. I have no idea how many British tanks were lost as they tried to scatter and retreat. There could have been as many as fifty or sixty lost, I didn't know for certain. As the counterattack of the Germans overwhelmed us, the tanks shelling our troops were killing dozens. Walls that had been built from brick or stone were collapsing all around us as they were hit by shells fired from the oncoming tanks. The fragmentation of brick and stone was coming down around us like rain. Then the word came down: "Retreat. Retreat!" It seemed like men were running everywhere as we retreated as quickly as possible.

When we had run all the way back to the area where we had made the river crossing, we were ordered to make a stand to hold off any further counterattack from that location. Our troops took cover, machine guns were set up, and anti-tank weapons were made ready. At this location we were out of that hellstorm of the Panzer attacks, but the battle was not over yet. We knew that at any moment we would be under another wave of German assault. As we looked to our south, we could see the battle still raging. We waited to see if the fighting would work its way north to our location.

Our squad was set up to defend from an intersection surrounded by fallen buildings. Tillins and I took cover behind collapsed stone walls. As I lay on my stomach, I set machine gun clips at an arm's reach so I had reloads ready to go. Tillins looked at me and said, "Hey, look at that." He pointed to a wooden observation tower that had been built by the Germans. It looked like it was built as an elevated observation point for controlling traffic at the bridge. It was elevated just enough so the traffic controller inside could see over the top of tanks and trucks. Tillins said, "I'm going up there." Before I could even say a word, he was up and headed for the tower.

When he got to the tower, he climbed up the ladder and stood on the platform that was about fifteen feet in the air. He looked back at me, smiled, and gave me the thumbs up. He then hollered, "I'll see them coming long before they get here."

We then had to wait and see what would happen. Not that far from us, we could hear the battle raging. Most of the tanks that had led us into battle had not survived. Other British troops that had attacked to our east were also being pushed back just like we were. To our west, the Canadians had run into the same kind of fierce resistance and were also being pushed back. The whole operation had become a huge disaster. It was obvious the Germans were well dug in on the high ground south of us, and they were very determined to hold that ground.

As a couple of our surviving tanks returned from that German hell-storm, they were directed into defensive positions and made ready to repel any further counterattack. Next, more tanks were moved up from our rear position to reinforce our position and knock out any attacking German tanks before they could fire on us.

It wasn't long until we saw something in front of us; there was enemy movement. At a distance, German infantry was moving up and taking cover. Tillins yelled, "Here they come." A moment later the shooting started. I looked toward the tower Tillins was in. I could see the wood start splintering, rupturing, and fragmenting as bullets ripped through it. Tillins dropped his rifle and fell on his stomach, covering his head. I hollered, "Tillins, get off of there! Tillins, come on, let's go! Jump … Jump! Come on, get the hell out of there, Tillins! Goddamn it, Tillins, get off that Goddamn tower!"

Goddamn it, he froze. My desperate yelling had turned into one desperate thought—*Christ, Tillins, you dumbass bastard.* Wood was still splintering and flying into the air. The Germans were getting closer and the shooting was picking up. Soon the bullets hitting the lookout tower wouldn't just be sporadic shooting. They would be accurate shots meant to kill Tillins. I thought to myself, *Damnit, damnit, this is bad, goddamn it!*

I don't know where the idea came from or what impulse got into me, but in an instant I was up and running toward the tower. Over the collapsed stonewall I went, and in seconds I was on the street headed for the ladder of the tower. Jesus Christ, I heard that goddamn BIZ! BIZ! BIZ! It was the sound of bullets whizzing close by me as I made my way toward Tillins. For a split second I remembered running across the deck of the LCT on D-Day. Goddamn it, I hated feeling such intense fear. Regardless, I kept running as fast as I could, knowing any hesitation on my part could result in my death. My thoughts were those of utter terror. *Goddamn it, this is horrible. I am so scared, it's pitiful.*

Within another few seconds I was reaching for the ladder. Then my hands and feet were moving upward as fast as they could. When I had made it to the top of the ladder and looked across the deck, I saw Tillins, shaking like a leaf and frozen like a rock. Splinters of wood were flying everywhere. I had no time to think or plan. All I wanted to do was get Tillins and then get the hell out of there. Using both my hands, I grabbed one of Tillins' legs at the ankle, pulled, and jumped off the tower.

I held onto Tillins' ankle all the way down to the ground. When my feet hit the ground, I fell to my side and rolled as I let go of my grip on Tillins' leg. I remember seeing him hit the ground in a horizontal position. He landed on his side and shoulder and then bounced, doing about a quarter turn in the air before landing on his back. I got up immediately, still hearing that BIZ! BIZ! BIZ! of bullets zipping by. I got up and gripped both of Tillins' ankles and, as quickly as I could, started dragging him to cover. He wasn't moving. *Oh no,* I thought, *if he wasn't already dead from a bullet, I must have killed him in the fall.* When I got within a few feet of the fallen stone walls, two guys came out and helped me pull Tillins to safety.

I immediately grabbed Tillins and pulled him close to me to see if he was breathing. Yes, he was struggling to inhale and he was making sounds of sucking for air. Thank God! Then he gasped and sucked in a strong intake of breath and started choking. I said out loud, "Thank God you're alive and I didn't kill you in the fall."

As he started breathing better, I checked him over to see if he was shot. He looked okay—no blood anywhere. It looked as though he was suffering from the worst case of getting the wind knocked out of his lungs that any man ever suffered. *Oh man*, I thought, *I'm so glad I didn't kill him in the fall.*

Then our squad sergeant hollered, "Bill, get your weapon and get on the line." I left Tillins and ran back to my machine gun. By this time the German troops were taking cover about two hundred yards from us and were quickly working their way closer. This time we didn't have to worry about being flanked, because our front was so wide it would be nearly impossible to flank it. We knew it was an inevitability that the fight would be coming from straight ahead of us.

As the German troops closed in, our reinforcement tanks moved up from the rear, firing rounds from their positions. It didn't take too many rounds from our new support tanks to repel the counterattack and send them back to the ridge south of town. When they had completely retreated, the British commenced with an artillery strike to drive the German tanks and their troops back even further to the south. The British also called in air support to further assist in driving back the counterattack.

As soon as we were out of danger, I ran over to see how Tillins was doing. When I got to where I had left him, he was sitting up against a large rock at the base of a fallen wall. He had gotten his breath back but still wasn't looking too good. The first thing I noticed was that he had blood coming out of both corners of his mouth. I said, "Hey, Tillins, how you doing?"

He looked at me and said, "You know, Bill, a fellow could get killed around here!" I couldn't believe it. Even in the face of death, Tillins was still the funny man. We both smiled a little. He started coughing and spitting up a little more blood. I told him not to try talking, that he should just rest and wait for the medics. He said they had been there already and that he was not a priority. They would be back to check on him in a few hours.

I sat with Tillins as we waited for the medics to come back. While he was dozing off, I went to get water for him. When he woke up, he gagged and coughed up a lot more blood as he cleared his throat. I gave him water and then we checked his side. He was already getting black and blue from the fall. I told him I felt pretty bad for pulling him off the tower the way I did. He said, "Don't you worry about that one bit; I'm glad you came out to get me. I would rather be hurt like this than be dead. No sir, don't you feel bad at all; you saved my life."

Later that night the medics finally got back to Tillins to take him to a field hospital. I helped load him onto a big military truck. When I got off the truck, Tillins looked at me and smiled. He said, "You know, Bill, a fellow could get killed around here!" With that the truck driver started the engine, and Tillins waved as they pulled out.

Over the next several days, we held our position by the river. We repelled several more German attacks with the help of air support and lots of artillery. The whole time, the ridge south of us was constantly being bombed by the British Air Corps and shelled by our artillery. Many of the British soldiers were sure no one could live through that kind of bombardment. I knew better than that. Many of the new reinforcements were also saying that when we attacked, there would probably be little resistance, that it was most likely going to be rather easy. Little did they know.

The next operation was being planned as we were again prepared for an attack to the south. The plan was that the military's air power would deliver several waves of bombers behind the Germans' frontline. That would divide the Germans' frontlines from their support, preventing their reinforcements from assisting the frontlines with re-arming and refueling during our attack. That way our forces would be cutting out one small group of Germans and defeating them. The overall battle plan for us foot soldiers was to support the tank crews. Along with our support, artillery fire and fighter planes would assist the tanks as they attacked the separated pieces of the German military. The tank attack was scheduled to begin after dark. This attack was different from anything the tankers had ever done before. They spent several days practicing in daylight on how they would attack and support each other in the dark.

When the attack commenced, we foot soldiers didn't play a large part in the operation. Our part was to move up behind the tanks, where we were held in reserve if needed. The cutting out and defeating of a small piece of the German army proved to be a very successful tactic. After the battle, we were moved for the purpose of securing the area. I remember participating in this sort of operation several times over a week or so as the Brits kept pushing the enemy further and further south.

The success of these operations gained a lot of ground on the southern side of Caen. We then pressed on and attacked the Germans who were positioned on the high ridges still further south of us. I was getting ready for this next operation, just like everybody else, when I heard a man say, "You know, Bill, a fellow could get killed around here!"

I turned around and there was Tillins. A wide smile gave away the pleasure I was trying to hide. "Hey, Tillins, how the hell are you? Are you okay? I didn't think you would be coming back. I thought you would for sure be on the way home."

Tillins said, "No, they said I had bruised lungs from the fall. I hit the ground so hard I jarred and bruised my lungs and was spitting blood. After a week or so of rest, I'm as good as new. My thigh, my side, and my ribs and shoulder were pretty black and blue, as well. But I'm ready to go again! The doctors told me I don't get to go home because I was a little bruised. They were joking with me, saying that I don't even get a Purple Heart, even though inside my chest I probably really had a purple heart."

I again told Tillins how sorry I was for pulling him off that tower the way I did, and that I never meant to injure him. "Don't you worry about that one bit," he said. "I might not be here today if you didn't come out and get me out of there. No sir, don't you worry one bit. I'm goddamn thankful you came to get me … really … goddamn glad."

Tillins was then refitted with new equipment. We were placed together within our infantry outfits and made ready with all the rest of the troops to attack the ridges to the south of Caen. Later that night when it got dark, our tanks led the attack to the south in columns, as they had been practicing for the past several days. Late that night we were transported through an industrial area to the south front on military troop carriers and trucks.

When we got close to the German front line, we were dropped off and immediately put to work in the dark, digging trenches in the powder-dry ground. During the night, the British set up thirty or forty huge spotlights over our tanks on the battlefield to provide them with a minimum of light so they were not in 100 percent pitch blackness. As we were lying in the trenches we had dug, we listened to our tanks battling with the Germans. That night was horrible for getting any sleep. Even those of us who were exhausted got little-to-no sleep at all because of the tremendous ground shaking and thumping as our artillery fired shells over our heads toward the enemy lines. As night turned into the first light of morning and the battlefield became more illuminated, the noise we heard coming from the battle became louder. From both the British and German sides you could hear tanks firing along with artillery blasts, mortar shots, and the squealing of rockets.

When the morning had reached full light, we could hear the sounds of our bombers pounding the enemy behind their lines in the distance. As we listened to the sounds of war, one of the distinctive and most prominent ones was the sound from those God-awful German 88s. It sounded as if they had a bunch of them.

By full sunrise we had not seen any close enemy movement at all. Our sergeant had us stacking extra sand bags and cutting light brush to camouflage our position. Then word came down that we were going to move forward. As we headed out on foot, we passed several wounded from other squads being transported back on Jeeps. Shortly after that, we came across several dead British soldiers. There were mutilated bodies lying everywhere, and tanks still burning and trucks and Jeeps up-ended from explosions, with their dead crews still in them. These dead soldiers spoke volumes about the battle that had unfolded hours earlier.

It wasn't easy following the terrain, because we were trying to avoid drawing small arms fire or being attacked with mortar fire. The first fighting we came across was in a factory's loading yard, where a German tank was dueling it out with one of our tanks. Both tanks were moving in and out of several storage buildings, trying to get a shot at the other. Both never slowed enough to become a target, but neither slowed enough to get off an accurate shot at the other either. Round and round they went.

Our Sergeant had two soldiers move in close so they could fire an anti-tank armament, a weapon that looked something like a bazooka, into the side of the German tank. That shot blew a track off of one side of their tank. With that shot, the Germans were killed in their tank. The British tanks quickly hit it with two shells, both direct hits. It exploded in a fiery inferno and burned without one German soldier ever exiting. We talked to the tankers for a few minutes and got their thoughts on the locations of any enemy troops in our area. They told us we could expect to find Germans setting up defensive positions almost anywhere in the immediate area. Then the Allied tank crew thanked us for our help and left us to continue on their patrol.

As we continued moving forward, we constantly looked for enemy positions. Suddenly, one of our British guys spotted three German helmets bobbing up and down in a small trench. The Brit hollered, "Halt!" As soon as they heard him, they stood up and raised their hands. I said to our sergeant, "Looks like we have three prisoners." We walked up to them. They were just three kids, probably about fifteen or sixteen years old. They were talking as fast as they could in German, with tears running down their cheeks, and they were shaking with fear. As I stood there listening to their pleas, I heard the ripping sounds of a machine gun come from behind me, and all three of them fell to the ground dead. Our sergeant walked up to me and said very loudly, "We don't take goddamn prisoners. If you don't shoot these no-good German bastards that have been killing good British soldiers, we're going to shoot you." I nodded, submitting to his reasoning even though I didn't agree with it, and I didn't say another word.

Not another word was said about it as we all fell into line and again started moving ahead looking for more enemy positions. As we were moving forward and coming out of some very large, overgrown hedgerows that led to an apple orchard, trouble hit us as the Germans opened up with mortar fire. The first mortar shells landed toward the rear of our squad, killing and wounding several of our troops. We were forced to run forward to look for cover. Fortunately for us, we quickly found shelter in some abandoned German trenches.

The enemy had our location under direct visual observation. They quickly started adjusting fire to better hone in on our exact location. When they had it, they started to rain down hell on us with extreme accuracy and determination. We had no other choice but to lie low in those abandoned foxholes as our radioman was calling in for help. As I lay on my stomach in that shallow trench, I could feel dirt raining down on me after each mortar explosion. I could hear the radioman's British accent spelling out the numbers and letters that represented our coordinates. A moment later he got a response and then he yelled out, "I got word that our artillery will commence firing on the ridge ahead of us as quickly as they can." Within a minute, artillery rounds started landing a hundred or so yards past the German mortar positions. Our radioman told our artillery they were over-shooting the ridge, and he gave them the adjustments needed to modify their fire.

When our artillery shells started landing on top of the German positions, their mortar shelling stopped immediately. We stood up in our trenches and watched the Germans as they were now having hell brought down on them. The British artillery was absolutely outstanding and knocked the daylights out of those poor bastards. Most of the German soldiers on that ridge were killed; only a few retreated and survived.

When we came out of our trenches, our guys immediately started taking care of the wounded. I'm not good with seeing people suffering or taking care of bleeding wounds. Considering that, Tillins and I volunteered to take care of the dead, as they were no longer suffering. When we were laying the dead bodies in rows, we came across the body of our sergeant. I immediately told our radioman to call command and let them know our sergeant was dead.

Later, several Jeeps showed up to take the wounded for medical care. A staff sergeant came from the rear with them to reorganize our squad. Naturally we all gathered around him to get our next orders. He first told us that we were going to stay there for the rest of the day and get some rest for a mission later that night. He went on to tell us that we would next be assigned to searching for a specific piece of 88MM artillery. He said that this particular 88 was well hidden by the enemy and was being used as an anti-aircraft gun. He then gave us a few details about the general area that command suspected that particular 88 was hidden in. Our assignment would be locating the 88MM gun so it could be destroyed.

The staff sergeant took all the soldiers who were remaining and reorganized us into new squads of ten men each. He then went from group to group to determine which groups needed a sergeant. As our squad stood waiting to have one of our guys assigned as sergeant, the staff sergeant walked up to us and said, "You … you're in charge of this group." I looked around to see who he was looking at. I thought he was looking at someone just behind me, so I turned to see who our new sergeant was. There was no one there. I looked left and right, and there was no one there either. *No, no … come on, not me,* I thought. *You can't mean me.* I looked at the staff sergeant and told him, "I can't be your sergeant. I'm an American."

He shook his head and said, "You're right, I guess I don't have the authority to promote you to be one of my sergeants. But I can tell you this—I do have the authority to put you *in charge*. So that's it. You're in charge."

"You know I'm not even in the army. I'm a sailor," I said.

"Shut your mouth," he said. "I know who you are—William Grannetino. And if I say you're in charge, then you're in charge. You're going to lead these other nine men in this squad. That is an order, so get ready because in a few minutes you're going to meet with me and the two other sergeants to get the details of this mission."

I just looked at Tillins and shook my head. Then I said to Tillins, "How the hell did I get put in charge?" He acted like a clown, just laughing, and he saluted me.

Still baffled by my recent promotion, I followed the staff sergeant along with two other sergeants he had selected for this assignment to his Jeep. We looked at maps and talked about what areas each team would cover during this search. We then went over the procedures we would use to search at night for a well-hidden 88MM gun. The staff sergeant finished our briefing by directing us to have our men get some rest so they would be alert as we searched later that night.

I went back to our guys after the briefing and relayed the plans to them, describing all the details of our assignment. When I was done, Tillins, "the clown," saluted me a few times and then said, "Yes, sir! Yes, sir! Sergeant sir!" The Brits sat back, made some tea, and then we all sacked out and got some sleep. When we woke up we could only see the last rays of light as the sun slipped below the skyline. We were issued food supplies and ammunition.

We filled our backpacks and grabbed our weapons as we headed out to begin our search for the hidden 88MM.

When we got closer to the front lines, we moved slowly along the hedgerows and through small fields and wooded areas. We would send one man out a few hundred yards as a scout to check for danger. When he returned, we would follow him to the end of his first track. Then we would do it again. The first night, we moved two or three miles toward the enemy-held ridge to our south. As we were moving, we could hear the sounds of the war in the distance. We heard tanks or trucks and would avoid those areas. If we saw lights, we worked our way around them as well. Before daylight, we dug in shallow trenches as we prepared to hole up for the day. Two men were put on lookout as the rest of us slept in our slip trenches. In the afternoon, all of us were well rested and wide awake as we just lay in our trenches, waiting. We had to stay put until nightfall before we could get up and start moving again.

Just before dusk, we heard something in the distance. It was the sound of Allied planes flying overhead about a half-a-mile or so from us. As we listened, we heard that shrill sound of a German 88 being fired. Immediately, all ten of us sat up and listened to that all-too-familiar squealing sound. Within a few seconds, the sound of flak exploding in the sky rang out. Sitting there with my left hand behind my left ear and looking up, I glanced at Tillins and he said, "That's it ... that's our gun."

Suddenly, everybody was standing up and listening. All of us talked about where the gun might be located. Then the scout and I made plans for the route we would take to move in closer to the 88 to figure out its exact location. I looked at the maps of the area, checking the terrain and considering the amount of cover that would be available as we made our way toward the target. After planning the path we would take, we waited for complete dark before moving out.

When the sky was finally filled with stars, we moved out slowly, just like the night before, always sending our scout out to check for activity before we moved as a group. After a few hours, we were in the area where we had heard the gun. It seemed vacant— no gun, no activity, no enemy. We talked about it and all agreed that this was the area for sure. After thinking about it more, we decided that the gun had been here but must have been pulled out before dark and was being redeployed somewhere else.

With the gun now assumed to be gone, I planned to head our group north to safer territory. The shortest distance back wasn't the path we had used to get there. That meant we would be moving slowly through new areas, just as we did to get there. We sent out our point man to check the trail before we all made our first move. When he returned, he quickly ran to me and said, "I found it! I found it! I found the 88! A few hundred yards from here, I was working my way along the side of a ridge and came to a set of railroad tracks. There is a train tunnel through the ridge there. The 88 is sitting on a flat railroad car hiding inside the tunnel."

Damn, was my first thought. I wish that goddamn gun had been pulled out and redeployed somewhere else. *Damnit! Now that we found it, we have to do our job*. I rounded everybody up and made a plan on exactly how we would move in closer.

An hour or so later we were hidden at the base of the ridge, about fifty yards away from one end of the tunnel. We could hear small noises coming from inside the tunnel. We watched and listened for a few minutes. To our surprise, the enemy had not posted guards outside the tunnel. I sent one man down to get a closer look. When he got back he said that there were two German soldiers sitting and talking quietly in the tunnel. The rest appeared to be asleep on the ground to one side of the railroad car that had the 88 mounted on it.

I told our fellows that we were going to move slowly and quietly to one side of the entrance. When we got there, we would lie on our stomachs and slowly crawl in front of the opening, lining up in a row on the ground so that we were looking down the tunnel. I said, "Once in place, we will prepare to fire our weapons only open fire when you hear me start shooting my machine gun." I added, "Do not stop shooting until you're empty."

One at a time, each man crawled and rolled his way in front of the tunnel. I was the last man to get into position. As I looked down the underground passageway, I could see moonlight at the other end of the tunnel. That was enough light to see the silhouettes of the two German soldiers who were still talking quietly. I pulled the trigger on my Lewis automatic and started firing down one side of the tunnel. On cue, everyone else opened fire. I could see sparks streaking through the dark as bullets ricocheted off steel as we fired. After the two soldiers fell, I continued firing, lowering my gun to the floor of the tunnel to take out the sleeping Germans. When I was empty, I stopped and waited for the last gun to stop shooting. A shot or two later, it was totally quiet.

We all lay there for several moments and heard only dead silence. Not a sound came out of the tunnel. I said, "Let's shine a light in there." One of the British immediately shined a light at the passageway. There was nothing moving ... nothing moving at all. It was completely still. "Okay," I said, "Let's get two men in there." I pointed at two fellows. "You and you, head in there slow." Without question, they were up and moving. They worked their way down one side slowly and disappeared into the darkness.

After a minute I heard, "All clear ... they're all dead." They turned their lights on as we were all getting up.

Tillins said, "Let's check this out."

"No way," I said. "Not me; that's not in my category. I'll stay here. You check it out." With that, Tillins headed in alone.

We had a demolition man with us who, as Tillins and I spoke, was already working to disable the 88 permanently. He placed thermite grenades in the correct locations to melt steel in such a manner that the barrel and firing mechanism of the 88 could never be repaired and used again. Everybody came out of the tunnel as he hollered, "All clear." As we watched, the chemicals inside the grenades burned white-hot, melting the steel permanently.

When the steel had stopped melting and burning, I said, "Let's get out of here before some Germans show up to see what all that shooting was."

We started back by the shortest and safest route we could take to friendly territory, again sending out a single soldier to check for enemy movement before we moved ahead. We moved slowly through the hedgerows, along small fields, and through wooded areas until we were again in a safe area.

When we got back I reported to the warrant officer in charge that we had completed our mission successfully. After taking our information, he immediately reassigned us to a very familiar task. He told us we would be clearing out houses door by door just as we had done in northern Caen. The warrant officer also said that we were going to be teamed up with several other squads in that next operation—the biggest difference being I was the one now in charge of our squad.

The next morning we found ourselves in a small French town in southern Caen. The major fighting in the area was over. Most of the enemy and their tanks had been pushed far south of there. We found mostly German regular troops hiding out in those small towns. They were pretty quick to surrender. Hardly more than a warning shot was needed. It seemed as if they had more than enough fighting and were glad to give up and end the hell. Unfortunately, that wasn't the case when it came to the S.S. soldiers. They would put up a fight no matter what the odds were. If we outnumbered them ten-to-one and had tanks ready to attack, they wouldn't surrender. In those firefights, we would throw so much ammunition at them that they didn't have a chance of surviving. Regardless, they usually chose to die.

It was also the same with the Hitler Youth. They would fight to the death rather than give up. When we came across a group of Hitler Youth hiding in a burned out stone home, we fired a few warning shots and a translator told them to give up. They didn't move or respond. A few of our soldiers moved in closer, expecting them to come out with their hands raised, surrendering. Instead, one of them fired a poorly aimed shot in our direction. After that shot, an infantry soldier armed with a flame-thrower burned them alive. It was a horrible thing to see, but it was either them or us.

One of the most dangerous problems we had when clearing out the German stragglers in southern Caen was the snipers. Those guys seemed to find a church-steeple or any other elevated building they could, and they would wreak havoc when they opened up. We had two or three British soldiers killed by snipers. When a shot was fired, everybody immediately took cover and then the hunt for the sniper would begin. Not one sniper we encountered ever survived.

We also had to consider the booby traps when cleaning out southern Caen. As the main forces of Germans were being driven out, they tried to slow down our troops by setting deadly traps. They usually wired a grenade to a door or put a tripwire somewhere a soldier would walk. Occasionally they wired a gun or something they knew the British would want as a souvenir. It didn't take long for our guys to realize that you didn't pick up "souvenirs." When it came to buildings, the guys watched every step and were very careful about opening doors as they searched.

After a couple of weeks of this cleanup duty, these small towns were liberated just like Caen had been weeks earlier. At this point in time, the main British and Canadian forces had moved south and east beyond the ridges that stood south of Caen. Both British and Canadian forces were now working with the Americans to push the Germans back to Germany. With short notice, the British fellows we had joined were put on transport trucks and moved to the front as reinforcements. After the farewells, Tillins and I were told to report back to our British staff sergeant for our new reassignment orders.

When we were walking over to see the staff sergeant, Tillins said that we would probably be heading back to the coast near Vierville. He figured LCT 9134(A) was busy unloading supplies onto the beaches at Omaha. No doubt we would be reassigned back to our LCT and spend the rest of the war unloading ships. "Yes sir," Tillins said, "easy street from now on. No more of this hell and being shot at!" Tillins looked at me and said, "You know, Bill, a fellow could get killed around here!" We both laughed a little. I thought to myself, *Boy, I sure hope he's right about heading back to LCT 9134(A) for cargo duty.* If only that had been true.

[CHAPTER 6]

A Break in the Fighting

When we got to the British Command Center, we went in and asked to see the staff sergeant. After an hour of waiting, we were told that the staff sergeant would see us. As soon as we went in, the staff sergeant put us "at ease" and told us we could speak freely. Tillins immediately said, "Well, I guess we are heading back to see Ensign Corker and rejoin our crew on our LCT."

The staff sergeant answered, "I thought so too. I checked, but I was told your LCT went back to England a few weeks ago to be stripped for parts." As he said that, I saw Tillins' face go blank and become somewhat pale.

Now both of us stood there waiting to find out if our next duty would be on the German front or somewhere else a little safer. Unfortunately, and completely to our surprise, the staff sergeant told us he had no idea where we were going. He did tell us that the British and Americans had now joined together in a unified front. He said he had been told that after this connection of the Allied forces was made, he was to send most of his American reinforcements back to their appropriate commands. Next he told us that the British units we had been fighting with were now working with the Americans in a joint operation to encircle a large group of Germans. He explained that because of that operation, right now was a very busy time for both groups and that we probably would have to wait a few days to get our orders.

Unfortunately for us, the Americans had not yet replied with any information on where they planned to send us, so we were on standby for the next day or two until the staff sergeant got that information. He said we should get some hot food and take this time to get some rest and relaxation. Finally, he told us to stop in once a day and check with one of the fellows in the front of his office to find out if our orders arrived. We were then given a place to bunk and put our gear. As we were leaving, the staff sergeant said, "William, you did a good job for me when you were out there, and I wanted to thank you for that." As a further show of appreciation, he firmly shook my hand as we were leaving.

After we left, we were met with a bunch of disappointments. The place where we were to bunk turned out to be a tent, and the hot food turned out to be cold sandwiches with no meat, just tasteless vegetables. Heck, we couldn't even get a cup of coffee, because all the British fellows drank was tea. We weren't upset about the accommodations, but a hot cup of coffee would have been just what the doctor ordered for two weary American sailors. Oh well, in a day or two we would be back with the rest of the American soldiers.

The next day we watched as lots of British soldiers from several different military divisions constantly came and went. It was very impressive how this British Command Center was continuously busy with activity. With nothing better to do, we got something to eat, rested, and then checked to see if our orders had come in. No orders today. Well, we would have to check again tomorrow. Two days stretched into three, and three into four. To pass the time, we walked around, drank tea, went without our coffee, and ate lousy food or British K-rations, which were not even as good as the lousy food. It was getting a little boring. Finally, Tillins and I were so bored we decided to do something for a change. We agreed that we were going to head into the French countryside and find a place to get some real food and maybe even some coffee. The first thing we had to do was find a ride. Tillins and I split up, each of us looking for some kind of transportation. I was making my way around the different British units trying to get a Jeep and wasn't having any luck.

Next thing I knew, I saw Tillins riding my way in a young French fellow's car. It turns out that this Frenchman spoke English and was going to use his car as a taxi to earn a little extra money. He and Tillins had already made a deal to give us a ride into the French countryside and then pick us up later to bring us back. I jumped in the car and we headed out. Tillins told me we would be paying a bundle for this ride and that this young fellow was only going to take us a few miles because of the French gas rationing. Regardless, the expense would be well worth it if it meant some decent hot food, coffee, and a break from boredom.

We got talking on the way and found out that the Frenchman was fascinated with us Americans. He asked all kinds of questions about the United States and Americans. I started calling him Frenchy. Well, Frenchy asked question after question. He wanted to know about cowboys, gangsters, movie stars, and anything American. We told him all kinds of nonsense and had a good time playing on how uninformed and unfamiliar he was with real American life. By the time we had gotten a few miles into the countryside, he thought we were very influential American personalities.

We asked Frenchy to take us somewhere to get a decent meal and maybe even some coffee. After riding for a while, we pulled up to a French pub. I had no idea where it was, but it was still intact and open for business, which meant it was certainly good enough for us. We got out of the car, and to our surprise Frenchy got out right along with us. I told him he didn't have to stay with us, that he could pick us up in a few hours. Frenchy said no way, he was going to stay with us; besides, he said we would need an interpreter. Unable to come up with a convincing counterargument, we headed into the pub together.

When we were inside seated at the bar and ready to order something, we found out the French had a food shortage and were under strict food rationing. The owner of the pub, who also spoke English, could see that we were somewhat disappointed. He then said to us, "You know, for the right price you could still get a very good meal, including meat from a chicken or a duck." We quickly agreed, negotiated a price, and paid him. Then we ordered chicken. In America we like to joke that if a restaurant is taking too long to bring a customer their food, it is because they are killing the animal out back. Well, that was literally the case in this French pub. After ordering some chicken, the owner sent his son out the back door to catch and kill a chicken. Soon we were drinking very strong French coffee and eating pan-fried chicken with a side of french fries, cheese, and bread and butter. At the time it seemed like it was one of the best meals I ever had in my life. The chicken was as juicy as any I had ever had, and the golden french fries smelled just like the ones back home that my father used to make. There was no beer to be had, so at the end of the meal we had wine and some kind of dry crackers to go with the wine.

After spending a few hours at the pub, Frenchy took us back and dropped us off. When we were getting out of the car, Tillins said to Frenchy, "Hey, pick us up tomorrow."

Frenchy replied, "I will pick up for the same price." Tillins agreed and then we headed over to the Command building and checked for our orders.

The next day Frenchy picked us up in the morning. "Where to, boss?" he said.

I answered, "Let's go to the coast and back to Vierville where we landed." Frenchy said that would take an hour and a half of driving one-way, and that would cost us a lot. We agreed on a price. Before we could go, Frenchy had to get extra gas from a couple of his family members. He put a can of gas in the trunk of the car. Before leaving, Tillins and I had stopped at Command and got our daily check-in out of the way. No orders today.

I said, "Okay, we'll check back with you fellows tomorrow." I told Tillins we were good to go.

We got on the road. The devastation we saw on the way was unbelievable. There had to be a couple of hundred vehicles of all types, mostly German, destroyed along the way. In one location the chassis of several German transport trucks were still smoldering. For the most part, any good American or British equipment had already been salvaged and put back in action with their damaged parts already replaced or repaired. The vehicles that were severely damaged were stripped of good parts that were quickly salvaged and reinstalled on another damaged vehicle somewhere.

When we got back to the Omaha section of Normandy, we could see that the beaches in the areas were now turned into several military cities. That didn't interest us all that much as we focused on making our way to the west side of Dog Green, where we stood talking about the hell we had lived through on the day we had landed there. After our visit to Omaha Beach, we went east along the coast so we could see the Mulberry Harbors at Arromanches on Gold Beach. It was just astounding to see how huge the operation of moving men and material had become over the last few months. After seeing the sites along the Normandy coast, we headed back through Caen. Caen was by far the worst area hit by the destruction of war. I don't think more than 5 percent of the buildings in Caen were untouched. For the most part, the other 95 percent were burnt-out shells or completely collapsed buildings.

After we were done retracing our steps through Normandy, Frenchy took us to another pub. For the first time in months we enjoyed wine, women, and song—mostly because that's all they had to offer. To say the least, we had quite a good time. Toward the end of the evening, Tillins noticed a dartboard. Soon we were playing darts, and Tillins was showing us how good he was by beating us at every game. When he would win, he would always say, "You know, Bill, a fellow could get killed around here."

We had used a lot of gas during the day. Frenchy had exhausted his and all his family's supplies of gas from their rationing and from his black market connections. It would be a while before he had gas again, so to help him out, Tillins and I, who didn't smoke, gathered our cigarette rations and bribed the British soldier in charge of fuel for a few gallons of gas to fill Frenchy's tank.

The next day when we were checking in on our orders, we were told that the staff sergeant wanted to see us. Tillins looked at me and said, "He must have our orders or he knows about the gas we got." We waited about an hour to see the staff sergeant. Finally, we were told he was ready. Next thing you know, we were in his office standing at attention.

The staff sergeant looked at us and asked, "Are you boys having a good time?" Before we could answer, he said, "I'm sure you are. I'm sure you are." Then he just stood there with his hand on his chin and looked at us for a few seconds. He told us that we couldn't forget there is a war going on and that there are men on the frontlines dying every day. Waiting for a reaction, he paused for a minute. We just stood quietly. He finally said, "I have temporary orders I'm going to give you gentlemen. You're going to be put to work doing something useful until your real orders come in." He said he knew I had specialized training, and he was well briefed and fully aware that I was a motor machinist mate. He said that was a good thing, because he could use a mechanic and his helper, and that, "Tomorrow morning both of you guys will be put to work. Dismissed." It seemed our break from the war would quickly be coming to an end.

The next morning a British soldier showed up at our tent and told us to gather our gear and load it into his Jeep. Tillins asked if we would be coming back that evening. He said that most likely we wouldn't be coming back, so we gathered our backpacks and weapons and we loaded up.

He took us to a captured German airfield that had been taken over by the British. We pulled up to a group of several buildings that were all shot up but still structurally sound. After grabbing our gear, the driver led us into a building where we met the sergeant who was in charge. He said, "Here are a couple of American mechanics. The staff sergeant said you should keep them busy working on trucks, Jeeps, or anything else you want." With that, he left and we stood there waiting for direction from our new sergeant.

First thing he said to us was, "How in the hell is it that I got two American mechanics?" Well, that triggered about a fifteen-minute conversation explaining how we got from the D-Day landing to there. When we were done explaining how we got there, the sergeant said, "Well, it's good to have you here; my name is Jack." After we introduced ourselves, Jack directed us to a tent where we stored our gear and weapons.

Next we were given something to eat, and then Jack showed us around. As we walked around we watched the bombers land and take off. It was amazing to watch them as they loaded their bombs. It was the closest we had ever been to such planes. We had seen planes like these flying overhead lots of times, but to be standing next to them was somewhat exciting.

As we watched I saw something very interesting—the pilots were having a problem with dust blowing up as they were getting into line for takeoff. They were not able to see when the aircraft was heading around to the end of the runway, so they had an aircraftman sit on the end of the one of the wings to be a second set of eyes for the pilots. When the pilots had gotten to the takeoff strip, the aircraftman jumped off and ran so that the next aircraft coming behind didn't hit him.

The motor pool we had been assigned to was set up in an empty hanger to the side of the airfield. A constant flow of trucks brought ammunitions from the coast to re-arm the planes. The convoys of ammunitions were only a very small part of the overall system of transportation that was in place for hauling supplies inland to support the troops fighting on the front lines. Sergeant Jack and his mechanics were helping to keep these trucks moving, as they were assigned to provide field maintenance for them. Within a few days, Tillins and I were just two more of Jack's mechanics. We were tuning up throttles, changing oil, repairing tires, and doing any sort of minor maintenance needed to keep the lorries moving. "Lorry," I had learned, is another name the British used for "truck."

After Tillins and I had been there for a couple of weeks, we started to wonder if the United States Navy had forgotten about us. We were guessing that some navy clerk had misplaced our paperwork and then totally forgotten they had sent us to the British as temporary reinforcements. Tillins and I agreed that this duty was pretty darn good, and if they forgot us for the rest of the war, that would be just fine with us.

From the D-Day landing until the time I had seen fighting in Caen, I saw hundreds, maybe even thousands, of planes flying overhead on bombing missions. At that time I had no idea how much support it took behind the scenes to sustain those bombing runs. Now being assigned to the motor pool and working from an airbase, I saw that support firsthand. I was amazed to find out the Royal Air Force (RAF) was using the bombers launched from here to support British and Allied Army troops all over Europe. The British aircraftmen told me that the RAF had also moved a couple of other bomber squadrons to other captured forward airbases in France, just like the one we were on. The pilots explained that it was their air support, along with the overall British and Allied air superiority, that was crucial to ensuring the success of all the Allied ground operations. These British pilots were quick to let us know they were reinforcing British, Canadian, and American forces, as all the Allied Forces were pushing the Germans out of France. They also told us they were now even beginning to fly missions into Belgium.

In my job as a motor pool mechanic, I didn't have anything to do with repairs of the aircraft. At a forward base like this one, the RAF handled their own maintenance and only did light repairs such as changing a tire, maybe tightening some loose nuts and bolts, or fixing up minor battle damage, but that was about it. When these planes had a mechanical problem, they would fly them back to England and have the repairs made by RAF-trained aircraftmen. A couple of times they had planes that were so damaged by flak that they crash-landed on the runway. The RAF ground crews would take care of fighting fires and cleaning up the mess after a crash. It was these same crews that would refuel and re-arm the planes for their next mission. Those fellows also had the duty of removing dead crew members when necessary.

The bombers at our location were basically just refueled and re-armed so they could fly quicker return missions over the enemy. The planes were never stored at that forward airfield when they were not actively flying missions; they were always flown back to England. Quite often, they would evacuate combat casualties on their return trips to England.

My job as a motor pool mechanic was totally unrelated to the RAF's aircraft duties. It just happened we were set up at the same place as the RAF. The outfit I was working with was focused on keeping supplies moving on trucks, and people moving in Jeeps. The only real interaction we had with the RAF fellows took place when we were eating, sleeping, and resting off-duty.

After a week of doing routine truck maintenance, our outfit was given notice that we would be assisting a British Recovery Outfit. The Recovery Outfits we would be working with were units of soldiers also under the same commanding officer as our group. The job of these soldiers was to clean up battlefields. They were always moving directly behind the frontlines. As soon as the fighting ended, they towed away heavy equipment that could not be repaired in the field and quickly overhauled them to get them back into action. They hauled the more excessively damaged heavy equipment like tanks, half-tracks, and armored cars to the crews trained to rebuild them and get them back into action.

Tillins and I were assigned to driving a lowboy-type tractor-trailer as part of a small convoy of trucks hauling vehicles off the battlefield. We were driving this flatbed as we headed to a yard full of knocked-out equipment that had been salvaged by the Recovery Units. Our assignment was to load two of those damaged trucks on our trailer and haul them back to our motor pool to be repaired.

Our convoy made its way along small country roads and through French villages. Along the way, we saw more bombed-out towns and lots of destroyed military equipment, including American, British, and German. This destroyed equipment was scattered along the sides of roadways, in open fields, and even in the towns we passed through. Most of the towns we passed through were badly damaged from previous battles, but occasionally we would pass through one that was totally untouched. At the end of our trip, we came to a field that looked like a junkyard filled with blown-up vehicles. There we had our trucks loaded by the Recovery Units, and immediately started our return to the motor pool.

I was driving as we were heading back to the motor pool, and Tillins was in the passenger's seat. About halfway through our trip home, as we were passing through a small French village, the length of our convoy was causing a small traffic jam on the narrow streets. We moved slowly as the locals waited for us to pass through when, all of a sudden, Tillins was out the window up to his waist yelling to someone. I could hear him talking back and forth with this person, but I couldn't make out what was being said. When he sat back in his seat he said, "What do you think of that?"

"Think of what?" I said.

"Frenchy," he said. "I saw Frenchy out there. I told him where we were now stationed. He said he would be by to see us some evening in the next week or so." That could only mean a good time was coming!

A couple of hours after that we were back at the motor pool and had our trucks unloaded. Sergeant Jack told us he was glad that we had plenty of work to keep us busy, and that it would ensure that he and the motor pool would remain working in a safe location. I thought this was for sure some great duty.

Now that we had those damaged trucks to rebuild, we would be doing a lot more than just general maintenance and oil changes. We now had the major task of completely rebuilding the trucks and getting them back into service. In some cases, we were taking two or three blown-up trucks, turning them into one completely rebuilt truck, and getting it back into the supply lines. When we were ready for more rebuilds, Tillins and I would take our lowboy and go for more trucks. We were constantly telling each other what a really good assignment this was, even if it was only temporary, while we waited for our new orders to come in. As Tillins put it, "Any assignment that doesn't involve getting shot at could only be considered a good duty."

A couple of days later on an evening in the fall, Tillins and I were walking back to our tent when we heard a car horn blowing from the far side of our tent camp, just outside of the entrance gate. We looked toward the sound and, sure enough, there was Frenchy. Frenchy was standing next to his car, waving his left hand in the air to get our attention while reaching into the car with his other hand blowing the horn. As soon as he knew he had our attention, he stopped blowing the horn and stood there with both of his arms held in the air like a winning athlete.

Tillins and I headed right over to Frenchy and greeted our friend with firm handshakes, acknowledgments, and warm smiles. After exchanging greetings, Frenchy immediately told us he knew of a local place where we could get some good food and drinks, but first he wanted us to see his new car. He proudly walked us around his car and showed us how it was equipped with a wood-burning furnace to make it run on a hydrogen and carbon monoxide mix of wood smoke. I had heard about these cars that could burn wood smoke, but this was the first one I had seen for myself.

It was amazing. It had a furnace that was a large steel tank that had air injected into a fire chamber for burning wood. The smoke from the fire chamber then was piped into a water-filled precipitating tank. The precipitating tank removed tars and most of the fine ash from the wood smoke. After that, the wood smoke was run through an automotive radiator for cooling. Next it went through a filter containing a fine mesh that was used to remove the last little bit of ash and dust before passing through the radiator. Finally, the refined wood gas was mixed with air in the regular carburetor and was then fed into the engine's intake manifold. Later I would learn that fine ash would clog the charcoal filter pretty quickly and reduce the smoke-gas flow. Somehow I ended up being the guy cleaning it regularly. I also inherited the job of stoking the furnace and shaking the furnace's grate as I had done before the war with our home coal stove.

"I didn't know it at the time, but twenty-five years later I would be designing a furnace to burn drain oil and would base some of that design on the technology I was learning from working on Frenchy's car."

-Bill Grannetino, 1998

After getting a good look at Frenchy's car, we decided to head out for a night on the town. As we ate and drank with Frenchy, he excitedly told us about the liberation of Paris. He described how thrilled the French people were now that their capital of France had been freed. He said he had been in Paris several times since the liberation and had seen lots of the festivities and celebrations. He said that he had been paid by a couple of different groups of American soldiers to take them to Paris during their leave. As soon as Tillins heard that, he said, "We'll pay you to take us to Paris."

Frenchy said, "No, no, no we are such good friends, you don't have to pay me; for you guys I will make the trip for nothing." We immediately decided that first thing in the morning we would talk to Sergeant Jack about getting some leave.

The next morning, as soon as we saw that Sergeant Jack was free, Tillins and I talked to him about getting some leave. The first thing he said was that he didn't know if he even had the authority to give anybody leave, let alone a couple of American sailors on temporary assignment. Then he said, "Besides that, what if your orders came in while you're gone? Then what would I do?" I said that he could just tell them that we're out hauling trucks back for repair, and when we got back, he could give us our orders and ship us out. The sergeant said, "I don't know."

"Listen Jack," I said, "Tillins and I have been doing a good job for you here at the motor pool. We've been making you look pretty darn good in front of your officers. Besides, we have hardly seen an American or had a decent American meal since we were assigned to assisting the British in

Caen. We have put our lives on the line for the British more than once. Don't you think the British Army owes us a little R&R for all we did over the last few months?"

Sergeant Jack scratched his head and then he closed his eyes at the same time he was shaking his head and gritting his teeth, clearly struggling with the idea of giving us leave. "Well, okay," he said, "but if you guys get into trouble, I'm telling them that you went AWOL and you forged your passes. You've got four days; you can pick up your passes in an hour." With that, Tillins and I were packing for the trip and were shortly on our way to Paris for a couple of days.

A couple of hours later we were in Paris. Frenchy set us up in a cheap hotel room far away from the main city. Our first impression of Paris was that it looked just like any other city in France—narrow streets with lots of quaint little buildings right up to the edge of their streets and no sidewalks.

A little old French woman owned the hotel Frenchy picked for us. There was a common bathroom for all the guests and a pitcher of water and a large bowl for washing in each room. She kept the rooms clean and would gladly make you a meal for a few cents if you first bought her the food to be cooked. We gave Frenchy money and he bought some food from the black market, because there still was a food shortage in Paris. However, somehow it seemed that there was always wine available.

That same evening we walked into the city to see the sites. Paris hadn't been bombed like Caen, so we had no trouble walking from place to place. As we walked toward the center of Paris, Frenchmen on the outskirts of the city were trying to lure us, as well as any other American soldiers, into girly shows, strip joints, or cheap brothels. There was no way Tillins was going to miss out on at least one girly show, so within our first few hours of touring Paris, we were in a strip joint watching topless women dance on stage. While standing there watching the girls, Tillins hit me in the ribs with his elbow. "Hey, I know her; I know her."

I asked sarcastically, "How do you know her?"

Tillins answered, "I saw her in the VD films they showed us in England." I shook my head and thought to myself, *only Tillins.*

After the show, we walked through the rest of the red light district. Frenchmen were standing in doorways trying to coax us into another show.

There had to be a hundred soldiers on the street taking in the same sites. MPs were everywhere, just watching and ready to keep rowdy soldiers in line. We saw a few groups of soldiers so drunk they could hardly walk. The whole place was like a carnival, with people walking up and down the street as if it were a midway, while hucksters were yelling and trying to get the crowd to spend their money. There were even people on the street selling trinkets like beads, costume jewelry, watches, and pocketknives. It was hard to believe that there was still a war on somewhere.

The next morning we were off early, heading for the Eiffel Tower. As we walked, we could occasionally see the top of the tower now and again due to Paris' rolling terrain and high buildings. We sure were glad Frenchy knew his way through the angled streets and how to get to the tower. Tillins had to clown around and keep asking Frenchmen along the way: "Do you know where the Eiffel Tower is?"

They would answer, "La Tour Eiffel" and point saying, "La Tour Eiffel, La Tour Eiffel." Tillins would thank them and then ask the next Frenchman the same question. As we got closer to the tower, we followed the swarms of soldiers heading toward the landmark.

When we arrived at the tower, I couldn't believe how huge and incredible it was—so much bigger than I had ever imagined. The weather was perfect for a breathtaking view of the whole tower as we walked up to it. I was hoping to climb all the way to the top of the tower.

Unfortunately for us, the tower was closed for security reasons. We wouldn't be going up to the top, not even to the lower sections. One of the Frenchmen guarding the tower did tell us some facts about the tower. The only two things I remember is that the tower was just around a thousand feet high and was made from wrought iron rather than steel.

Tillins, Frenchy, and I stood at the tower's base and talked about how only a few months earlier, there had been German soldiers walking around the tower just like us. More unbelievable than that was the fact that Hitler himself had also been there during the beginning of the war to see that unbelievable structure.

After seeing the Eiffel Tower, we decided to head for the next attraction. We crossed over the Seine River and headed north along some huge streets in Paris that were lined by very large three, four, and five-story buildings. As we walked, I do remember being surprised at how many horse and buggies there were along the streets. Other than military vehicles, there were more horse-drawn carriages than cars or trucks, due to the French gas shortage.

Frenchy told us we would next be going to see the Arc de Triomphe, an arch-type structure that was built about a hundred years ago to commemorate those who fought for France in the French revolution and the Napoleonic Wars.

I remember walking down a long road lined with double rows of trees on both sides of the street. As we came to the monument, I could see that it was set in a round intersection of eight or ten streets coming together at one main intersection. The arch was about fifteen stories high and cars could drive right through it. It was awe-inspiring and truly impressive, especially with the several massive carvings and its detailed engravings.

Under the Arc de Triomphe is a tomb known as the "Tomb of the Unknown Soldier," which was put there by the French after World War I.

During the rest of our leave we toured old churches, cathedrals, government buildings, and bridges, and took time to see several outdoor scenic views. At night, we went to see some military entertainment. We spent time in the bars and a night at the movie theater that was set up in English for the soldiers. We were most interested in the newsreel at the movies because we really had no idea what was going on at home and, especially, what had been happening in the Pacific Theater. Finally, on our last night in Paris, Tillins insisted we see one more burlesque show.

On that last night we headed back down to the red light district. We were again touring as Frenchmen tried to lure us into every strip joint and cheap brothel there was. After checking out all the possibilities, Tillins picked the show he wanted to see based on the girls they brought out front between shows. As Tillins watched, he scratched his head and then closed his eyes while rubbing his hands together; next he was turning his head to the right and then left as his eyes never left the girls. Finally he said, "Okay, this is the one—let's go." In we went and stood in a crowd of other yearning young soldiers. For the next half an hour, we watched topless women dance on stage to the applause of a crowd.

When the show was over, Tillins loudly raved over all the girls in the show as we headed back out to the street. By the time we were in the middle of the street, Tillins was really on a roll. He was laughing and joking as he made all kinds of lewd hand gestures, reliving the performances he had just seen. Soldiers on the street were even stopping and watching as Tillins rudely impersonated the exotic dancers. The next thing you knew, a small crowd had gathered to watch Tillins as he began enthusiastically impersonating one of his favorite dancers, an extremely-large breasted woman. As the crowd laughed hilariously, I'm sure some of those soldiers watching thought Tillins was getting paid by the promoter of the show.

Then out of nowhere two American MPs walked up to Tillins and stood face-to-face with him. Tillins immediately stopped his imitations and got quiet. He just stood there with a blank face and his mouth hanging open, waiting to hear why they were confronting him. The crowd quickly disappeared, not wanting to be a part of any trouble. I immediately came over and stood next to Tillins and asked the MPs, "Is there a problem here?"

The taller of the two stared directly into Tillins' face and said sarcastically, "We don't like the way you're standing out in the crowd, and for that reason, you're getting a routine check. Now let me see both your passes."

"Sure," I said, as we both pulled out our passes from Sergeant Jack. The taller MP looked at the passes for a minute or so and then said, "Wait a minute. What the hell are you guys trying to pull here? These passes are British." I started to explain that we were U.S. Navy guys assigned as reinforcements to a British infantry unit when they were in desperate need of reinforcements for taking Caen. Before I could finish, the MP again said, "Wait a minute. What the hell are you guys trying to pull here? What are you trying to tell me? You expect me to believe you are United States Navy sailors, and you have been fighting with the British infantry? Sounds like a bunch of bull to me. I think you guys are going to have to come with us; you have a lot of explaining to do. Looks to me like these papers are forged, and you guys could be deserters. I think we have ourselves a couple of cowards here."

Before I could say a thing, Tillins was face-to-face with this young MP. He put his forefinger against the MP's chest and with each word he poked him. "Cowards! Cowards! Who the hell are you calling a coward, boy? No man, no man, I mean no goddamn man in this goddamn world calls us cowards. You goddamn no good sons-of-bitches, I'll have you know on

D-Day we landed on Omaha Beach thirty minutes before the infantry arrived, and we were goddamn near blown out of the water. In Caen, we fought street-to-street with the British infantry for weeks and had our asses under fire more times than I care to think about. You no-goddamn-good-for-nothing bastards can harass us, you can challenge our passes, but if you call either of us a coward again, I'll gladly go to the brig for knocking a no-goddamn-good-for-nothing-coward-son-of-a-bitch like you on his ass."

The tall MP shoved Tillins backwards. Immediately the shorter MP and I jumped between them before they went to blows. We pushed them apart and fought to hold them back and shut them up. The second MP turned to me in a panic and asked, "Is what you're saying really true?"

"Yes, yes, it is. It's true, it's true, every word of it, and yes the passes are good."

"Okay, get him the hell out of here now—right now! Go … just go. No questions asked, just turn and go … go now … leave, leave."

I pushed Tillins along as he was still muttering profanities under his breath. Two or three times he turned around and challenged the MP to call us cowards again. Frenchy joined me in holding Tillins as we headed back to our hotel room. As we walked, Tillins kept telling us how he would have torn that guy to pieces if I hadn't jumped in between. Frenchy and I just shook our heads.

The next morning we made the trip back to the motor pool at the airfield. When we arrived we saw a noticeable change in activity. The British motor pool's equipment was being loaded onto trucks. "What the heck is going on here?" Tillins said. We headed over to see Sergeant Jack to find out what was going on.

"We are being moved closer to the front," he explained. "The Allied troops are getting so far to the north and east of us, it's becoming difficult to support them from here. I was told you two fellows will be staying here until your orders come in. Now get into your work clothes and help us load this stuff up."

Within a day, Sergeant Jack and the motor pool were gone. Tillins and I were assigned to Airfield Command and directed to keep busy doing odd jobs around the airfield until our orders came in. During an average day we would burn trash, unload supplies, clean up storage buildings, or do any other jobs that were unrelated to the planes. The whole time we were there, we had lots of slow time to just watch bombers land, reload, and take off again.

One evening as we headed back to our tent to clean up and get some rest, we found two envelopes lying on our bunks. I said, "Finally, our orders are here."

Tillins said, "Boy, I'm hoping I get assigned to a slow-moving cargo ship and spend the rest of the war hauling supplies across the English Channel." We opened up the papers and read quickly, looking for the location of our next assignment.

Tillins said, "Le Harve. Le Harve, France. Where the hell is Le Harve, France? I'm assigned to a supply unit shipping supplies out of Le Harve."

I said, "Looks like we're both being assigned to some sort of an American transportation unit and we'll be on a truck tomorrow headed for Le Harve."

Tillins said, "Thank God. I don't think I could take another day of eating this British food."

[CHAPTER 7]

From Le Harve to the Battle of the Bulge

THE NEXT MORNING, A TRUCK set up as a troop carrier arrived. Tillins and I loaded our gear into the back of the truck and headed for Le Harve. As I remember it, we made the trip westward toward the coast on a cool autumn day. The trip took us around seven or eight hours, because we stopped along the way a few times to pick up other soldiers who were also being reassigned to Le Harve. We finally arrived in a newly set-up tent camp when the sun was already deep into descent toward the horizon. We were all pretty tired, getting cold and rather hungry from that long ride. We were hoping to get warmed up and find something good to eat in an American mess hall.

Well, it seemed good luck was not going to be looking our way, as that's not the way it turned out. We were told we had to first get ourselves set up in our new quarters and equip our tents before doing anything else. We were issued cots, blankets, a small coal stove, and a bucket. Then we were directed to our new homes in this canvas city of tents, which all had pyramid-shaped roofs. After finding our tent and setting up our new living quarters, Tillins took our new bucket and hauled coal from the camp's community stockpile. As soon as he returned with the coal, I stoked a fire in our new little potbelly stove while Tillins filled the bucket with water and placed it outside the front flap of our tent. We had been directed to do that as a precaution in case of fire.

Now that we had our living quarters set up, we went looking for the mess hall so we could finally get some decent American food. What we found was a supply tent that was handing out K-rations. The soldiers handing out the K-rations and other supplies told us that there were plans for setting up a mess tent, but it was still a few days away. Tillins and I heated canned meat over a coal stove, made powdered coffee, and ate crackers. We finished our meal with a chocolate bar. It was hardly the meal we had envisioned, but it was enough to put our aching stomachs at ease.

After we ate, we talked to the sergeant in charge. He told us that in the morning we were going to be assigned to a supply outfit as truck drivers. Knowing that, we returned to our tent. I stoked our coal stove, and we turned in early.

The next morning, we woke up to the harsh realization that our fire had died in the middle of the night, and we shivered as we quickly got up and put on our coats. Tillins headed for the supply tent to get some morning K-rations. As soon as he stepped out of our tent, I heard him complaining under his breath about how cold it was outside. By the time he got back, I had a small wood fire burning in the stove just to push a little chill out of the tent. For breakfast, we again heated canned meat on the stove and also ate some ridiculously dry biscuits.

We joined up with the rest of the new reinforcements, assembled and loaded into trucks heading to the harbor front. When we arrived there, a lieutenant asked each one of us about personal training and our individual experiences that related to driving large trucks. When it was my turn to respond, I told him about my diesel schooling and LCT training and the experience I had with the British motor pool. His first response was, "I don't understand how a sailor got to see the duty you described or how you ever ended up here, but I sure need qualified truck drivers and I'll take anybody they send me." He then said that with the experience I already had, they wouldn't need to be giving me any driving lessons, and that I would immediately be assigned to hauling supplies inland. As I walked away, he said to one of his sergeants, "This guy apparently has experience with bigger trucks. Don't put him in a duce-and-a-half. I want him assigned to one of those bigger Diamond T Prime Movers they sent us. He'll be able to shift a heavily loaded truck on steep grades. I want him to be one of our ammunition and tank haulers. Team him up with his tall, skinny friend there."

Hearing that, Tillins looked at me and said, "Thanks a lot. That's just what I wanted—to be driving around in a war zone in a truck loaded with explosives."

The Diamond T was a massive twelve-ton truck with an engine that was over 1,000 cubic inches in size. It was a straight 6-cylinder gasoline engine that had pistons the size of paint cans. It had a twelve-speed transmission and was equipped with airbrakes. These trucks were designed to pull a trailer loaded with the heaviest of tanks or to carry the heaviest loads of ammunition.

When the lieutenant was done assessing the qualifications of all the new truck drivers, he briefed us on the duties we would be performing for the next few months. The first thing he said was, "You'll be driving your trucks round and round and round northern Europe until you're dizzy." He went on to explain that our job would be to supply the Allied troops with whatever they needed as they were driving their way into Germany. "You will be hauling bullets, missiles, bombs, grenades, fuel, food, clothes, first aid supplies, and whatever else those brave boys at the front need to win this war!"

Then the lieutenant told us about the organized truck convoy system that had very recently been created to supply our frontlines by moving quickly and efficiently through Europe as they followed our troops fighting eastward. He explained that the army was hauling supplies from the coast of the English Channel to distribution areas just behind the frontlines. He went on to tell us that now that the Le Harve port was open, the Allies' trucks would become part of a newly created trucking system carrying supplies east to mainly Rouen and Reims, France, into other areas of northern France and Belgium— and even some trips to railheads in Paris.

The Lieutenant finished the briefing by telling us two things. First, that a large percentage of our drivers would be Negro troops. He warned us that any type of slander toward the Negroes would be dealt with harshly. Second, he told us that the civilians around Le Harve were very upset with the Allied armies about the excessive bombing the Allies used to drive the Germans out of Le Harve. He said there had been several confrontations between the locals and military personnel because of that. One of the most recent events was an incident in which civilians threw rocks at the truckers entering and exiting the harbor front. The lieutenant then warned us that we were not to retaliate in any way if that happened to us.

By the time all the new recruits had their personal training analyzed and each one had been interviewed about their individual experiences, it was well past midday. The lieutenant then sent us back to our tents in the tent city, where we ate a late lunch of K-rations and hot coffee. After about a forty-five-minute break, we were reassembled and taken back to the harbor front.

Those of us who were predetermined as qualified truck drivers without additional training were directed to our trucks. We were organized into small convoys of ten or twelve trucks, each with a Jeep escort. Then we were directed to the harbor front, where we took our place in a long line of trucks waiting to get loaded. As I was sitting there looking around, I could see that with so many trucks being loaded, it would be several hours until the line moved far enough along for Tillins and I to get loaded.

As I sat behind the wheel of our Diamond T truck waiting for the first freight to be loaded, I stared out the front window and saw the tremendous amount of destruction that the harbor had sustained during the liberation of Le Harve. That's when the driver of the Jeep who was escorting our convoys came up to our truck and told me that the Germans had destroyed 90 percent of the port facilities, sinking over a hundred ships and boats before evacuating. They had done everything they could, hoping to prevent the Allies from using this port. He said it was just recently that the Seabees had restored portions of the harbor for partial use. He pointed to the portion of the harbor where the Seabee crews were now starting to increase the depth of the Channel by dredging the entrance and several of the main dock areas. He also pointed out that several of the boats now floating at the docks were previously sunk by the Germans but had been recently repaired and refloated.

The rest of the harbor reminded me a lot of the Mulberry Harbors at Omaha Beach that had been destroyed by that horrible gale. Here at Le Harve, I could see that there were also several newly constructed floating piers and ramps being used for shuttling personnel and supplies directly from ship to shore. In other areas around the harbor, amphibious vehicles were being used to transfer cargo from ships to shore. As soon as the cargo had arrived on shore, it was stocked in storage areas and then later loaded on trucks to be moved inland.

Finally, late in the day when the sun was just about gone, the truck Tillins and I were driving was loaded with enough artillery shells to level a small city. Most of the other trucks in our small convoy were loaded with 5-gallon fuel cans. Still others carried oil, K-rations, medical supplies, and other essentials. Now with our whole group loaded, I assumed the officers in charge would have us park our trucks for the night and head back to camp for some food and sleep. To my surprise, our Jeep escort did his final organizing of our convoy and then announced that we would be pulling out shortly. A couple of the other drivers asked about getting some food and sleep before we left Le Harve. Our escort admonished, "You boys have to realize there are men at the front that are in harm's way and they're depending on these supplies to stay alive, so saddle up because we're headed east to the front to support our guys. Their success depends on us, and we will not let them down. If there are no other questions, we pull out in five minutes."

Our convoy left Le Harve with a total of two Jeeps for escorts. One Jeep took the lead and the other followed at our rear. The lead Jeep was staffed with two MPs and our escort, and the second Jeep was staffed with two MPs. It was quite clear from the beginning that the escort and the MPs were completely in charge of the convoy and fully responsible for our supplies being delivered safely and in a timely manner. They did all the mapping out of our convoy's route, which started at Le Harve, went to our delivery point, and back again.

We traveled along the roads just as we had been instructed during our brief training. When driving, we maintained a fifty-to-sixty-yard interval between trucks, while never exceeding the maximum speed of thirty-to thirty-five mph, and we fully complied with the no-passing-allowed directive. As a stark reminder to the ever-present danger surrounding us, Tillins and I, along with the other drivers, were given a short-barreled carbine to keep in the cab of the truck, and we were instructed to wear our helmets at all times. We quickly realized that night driving would be difficult. The truck's headlights were masked to narrow "cat's eye" slits so the convoy couldn't be spotted by our lights and subsequently attacked.

After our first hour on the road, the MPs stopped the convoy and instructed us to take a ten-minute break to stretch our legs and go to the bathroom. This routine was maintained every hour for all convoys. As soon as we were back on the road, Tillins and I decided to take off our helmets while inside the truck. When we were hungry, we ate cold K-rations in the truck. When our fuel got low, we added fuel from 5-gallon cans during our stops. We drove all night and into the next day.

When we finally reached our delivery point at an ammunition depot, we were just behind the American artillery positions and within a few miles of the front lines. The artillery humpers unloaded our trucks quickly and immediately reloaded us with salvaged shell casings for our return trip. As soon as all the trucks were reloaded, our escort and MPs took the lead as we started back to Le Harve. Tillins and I were now getting tired and started to catch catnaps in the truck as we switched off driving during our ten-minute breaks. We were looking forward to getting back to Le Harve and getting a couple of hours of sleep and some hot food and coffee.

Finally, after a very long trip, we arrived back at Le Harve. Our escort led our convoy down to the harbor and directed us back into a line of trucks to be reloaded. I told Tillins that we would most likely be loaded and then finally park our truck. We could then get some food and some sleep. We would probably leave again in the morning for another run. After we were loaded, I asked our escort where to park the truck. He told me to get in line with the rest of our convoy, and that we would have a new escort ready to lead us on our next trip in short order. Tillins asked the escort, "When will we be leaving?" He told us that we should be on the road in about twenty or thirty minutes. Tillins' face went blank. Then he asked the escort, "Hey, what about a little sleep and some hot food?"

The escort responded, "Forget hot food and plan on sleeping in your truck when the other guy is driving. Now get moving."

There was indeed fire in Tillins' eyes. I think it took everything Tillins had to bite his tongue. Tillins and I quickly found out what it meant to be cooped up in an ammunition truck with no hot food and little rest for days on end. This was an around-the-clock job. For the next several days, Tillins and I drove our truck at least twenty hours a day, stopping only for loading, unloading, and maintenance, with the ten-minute breaks each hour. We were constantly exhausted, only sleeping in the truck when the other guy was driving. After the first few days, Tillins and I, along with all the other drivers, had become so fatigued our escorts realized someone was going to have an accident if we didn't get some quality rest. We were told that as soon as we got back to Le Harve, there would be a break. I can still remember thinking to myself, *Thank God they finally recognize the fact that we need a few hours of sleep in a real bed.*

After our next return trip to Le Harve, our escorts told us to park the trucks and get some rest. We immediately headed to our tent. We didn't bother to spend what little energy we had on trying to start a coal fire; we just lay down on our cots, fully dressed, and went to sleep. After about four hours of sleep, they woke us up. We ate a hot meal and took a lukewarm shower. When all was said and done, we had about a six-hour break. While we were on our break, the harbor crews had reloaded our trucks and had them lined up in another small convoy, ready to go. So it was back on the road for several more days of round-the-clock driving. There was no rest for the weary, it seemed.

After a couple of weeks working as truck drivers, we started learning the tricks of the trade from more experienced drivers—like heating canned food on the manifold of our engine to get a hot meal. We also learned how to cook up K-rations and make hot coffee by burning gasoline in a tin can. Even beyond that, Tillins and I learned how to switch seats while the trucks were still rolling. One of the best things I heard about, and then did myself, was modify our truck's carburetors and disable the governor. In that way I was capable of traveling at speeds reaching fifty-to-sixty mph. As it turned out, we never used that capability anyway. Regardless, the real advantage to this was that we had more power on the hills and could run up hills in higher gear. That was especially helpful when our truck was loaded with heavy ammunition boxes that reached sometimes twice as high as the top of the truck, while at the same time pulling a heavy tank on our trailer. Before I had disabled the governor and increased the fuel going to the carburetor, the duce-and-a-half trucks would have to stop and wait for us as we slowly crawled up steep hills in low, low gear.

As truck drivers, Tillins and I were thankful that we had never needed to get involved in any combat. We were told that there was a danger of being strafed by Luftwaffe fighters, but we never even heard of anyone having seen a German plane. The worst hazards we ever saw on the road were farm animals roaming loose. The saddest sights to witness were starving French people who would stand on the side of the road and then run alongside our truck, begging for food. That made me feel horrible.

At times we were within miles of the front lines. On a few occasions we brought artillery shells directly to the crews firing their guns toward enemy positions. Tillins said that anytime we were that close to the front lines, he was uncomfortable. My overall opinion was that this was a good job. It was hardly exciting. It had endless hours of dull, exhausting driving, but it beat the hell out of getting shot at.

Weeks slowly turned into months, and by that point all the fallen leaves had a fresh coating of frost each morning as fall turned into early winter. During this period, we started having damper and colder weather. Temperatures were much cooler at night and we had lots of rain and fog. For the most part, we delivered supplies to depots in Belgium or to the Paris railheads. On return trips, our trucks were always loaded with something. A few times, the duce-and-a-half trucks in our convoy hauled wounded soldiers or even German POWs.

The worst thing we ever hauled was the remains of the dead being carried back from the frontlines to rear areas for processing. That job was a particularly dreadful task. I remember the awful odor of death that took days to dissipate from our trailer. We hosed down the trailer bed, but even after a thorough washing away of the blood and grime that oozed down through the cracks in the wooden bed, the stench remained for a while.

Tillins and I would never forget one particular trip we had made to a captured airfield in Belgium. The Americans were using it to launch short-range bombing missions. This was one of a couple of captured airfields in Belgium that we sometimes supplied with ammunition. It was around 0300 or 0400 as we were traveling along a small country road when our truck started steering hard. *Oh boy*, I thought, *I'm losing air in one of my front tires.* Within a few seconds I could hardly steer the truck and had to pull over. As I was stopping, a couple of other trucks in the convoy also pulled over with their own tire problems. It appeared that a few of our trucks had one or more flattened tires. Because the only light we could safely use on the roadway was our narrow-slitted headlights, our convoy had not seen that the road had been littered with chunks of steel. This steel came from destroyed military equipment, shell fragments, and other junk from a recent battle that had taken place on this section of road.

Our MPs and our escort immediately surveyed the tire damage on all the affected trucks in our convoy. Several of our trucks that were in the front of the convoy had one or two flat tires, or at least leaking tires. The escorts quickly decided that the men in trucks with one flat tire would change it using their own spare, which the trucks were carrying. Next it was decided that the men in trucks with two or more tire problems would change tires with their spares and use spare tires from the trucks without any tire problems. When all the tire changing had been finished, all the duce-and-a-half trucks in our convoy were ready to get back on the road.

Tillins and I were out of luck driving a Diamond T truck and trailer loaded with ammunition. First, we had more than two flats on the truck, and second, we had a couple of flats on the trailer. Because of our different sizes, we couldn't borrow tires from the fellows driving the standard duce-and-a-half trucks. After a full discussion between us, the MPs and our escort, it was determined that, as heavy as the truck was, towing our truck to a maintenance depot wouldn't be practical. That meant that we would have to wait for a repair crew to come and repair our tires. After about an hour of waiting, we found out that the tires and repair crews were to arrive late that evening. Tillins and I were thrilled to have this time off. We immediately planned to spend that down time sleeping in our truck.

By first light in the morning, all the trucks that had their tires changed were ready to get back on the road. It was soon light enough that we were able to help clean up the road so no other convoys would run into trouble. When we had finished getting all the trucks in the convoy on their way, Tillins and I were left waiting for our tires to be repaired. We were told that when our tires had been fixed, we would be joining another convoy, eventually returning to Le Harve with them.

Both our escort and the MPs knew that locating a repair crew this close to the front *and* locating several tires for a bigger Diamond T Prime truck was going to take considerable time. Knowing that, the MPs did something really admirable. They decided that Tillins and I could ride in one of their Jeeps for a couple of miles to the airfield where our cargo was originally going to be delivered. There we could get a hot meal and some rest. A couple of additional MPs showed up to guard our truck and its cargo to prevent some con-artist Frenchmen or any crooked American soldiers from taking anything that wasn't tied down. When we got to the airfield, we ate lots of very good hot food in a warm, dry building, then lay down on cots with padded cushions in a room with heat and got some needed sleep. Oh my God, it was like heaven compared to our normal living conditions. Regardless of all the good food and comfort, by midday we were awake and walking around watching the planes being armed for their next bombing runs. It was a welcome break. It was the first time in weeks that we were rested and had some leisure time.

We got talking to an army airman and told him about how we worked with the British at another captured German airfield. At some point in the conversation, he told us they would shortly be loading their next series of planes for low-level bombing runs, or what they called "hedgehop" bombing runs. He went on to explain that the planes they were reloading would be flying over the frontlines of the Germans and dropping bombs right in their laps. Tillins and I were amazed as he and the other airmen talked about these missions. They told us that a few of their ground guys had hitched rides on some of these missions. On and on they went, telling us how amazing it was to watch the chaos on the ground as the Germans scrambled to survive these missions. Those were amazing stories about the complete devastation of tanks, artillery, and troops from these low-level bombing runs. "Yeah," one of them said, "it's for sure, hedgehop bombing is going to end this war a lot quicker."

As we continued to talk, I told them that when Tillins and I were at the British airfield, we were never allowed to even get near the planes on the British base, let alone go on one of the bombing missions. After listening to several more minutes of their miraculous stories of success, an older airman asked us, "Would you guys like to hitch a ride with us on one of our B25 missions flying today? We have a couple of planes that will be flying a hedgehop bombing mission this afternoon. We could probably get you on one if you would like."

I said, "Yes, we would! Of course we would! That is, you know, only if it isn't a problem for you fellows or your pilots. I don't want to ask you to do anything that would get you in a bind."

Immediately the older airmen said, "No problem, no problem. I'm sure we can get you guys on one of our planes flying a short mission today."

Less than an hour later, we were on a fully-armed B25 as it taxied down the runway. Tillins and I stood at the small porthole windows on either side of the plane looking out, waiting to experience flying for the first time in our lives. Tillins looked at me and said, "Boy, this is going to be something." The plane turned 180 degrees at the end of the runway, gunned the engines, and quickly started picking up speed as it accelerated. When we got about halfway down the runway, I felt the plane lift off. What a feeling! We were flying! This was something really special for a young kid born in the 1920s in a small town in Pennsylvania. I don't think I moved my face from the window for at least fifteen minutes. Everything looked amazing from the air. Woods, buildings, trees, fields and the different perspective of rolling hills and valleys was just amazing. After circling the airfield a few times, we joined four other B25s and headed east for a hedgehop bombing run intended to stop the advancement of German troops in a given area. The primary target would be a key bridge held by the enemy and also any other available military targets in the immediate area. There were two fighter planes flying ahead of the bombers to escort us and offer protection if needed.

After several minutes of flying, one of the pilots saw something in the distance. It turned out to be a couple of German fighters. Immediately our fighter plane escorts flew toward the enemy planes, intending to engage them. From a great distance we watched planes spinning and rolling as they shot at each other. One of the German fighters flew off, crippled. Then, just as quickly as it had started, it was over as the second enemy fighter retreated. I figured that the German fighter pilots determined they were no match for our American fighter pilots and decided to save their planes and their lives. Tillins looked at me and I looked at him. He shook his head and said, "Wow! That was something to see, wasn't it?" I just nodded my head and agreed.

A few minutes later the side gunner and rear gunner on board opened up with their machine guns. That second German fighter hadn't really given up ... he had just taken a huge loop to avoid the fighters and was attacking our bombers from a different angle. The violent concussions of the machine guns firing echoed around inside the plane, making it all but impossible to hear anything else. I looked out the window to see our fighters coming back to protect the bombers. The shooting inside our plane changed from machine gun to machine gun, from side to side, and from front to rear. The rotating shooting lasted only a minute or two as our fighters re-engaged the single enemy fighter. Because the fighters were so much closer to us, we could only see bits and pieces of what was happening when they passed in view of our windows. All the shooting from inside the plane quickly stopped as we flew away from that engagement. I couldn't believe it— in all that shooting we hadn't been hit with a single bullet. More surprising to me was that from all those rounds that were fired from our bomber and all the other bombers combined, not one had hit that enemy fighter.

Tillins looked at me and asked, "Whose idea was this?" All I did was shrug my shoulders, indicating *I don't know*. At that moment there was a huge explosion. Tillins' eyes opened wide and his face went white. Then a second explosion occurred and the whole plane shook, almost knocking us off our feet. Tillins desperately hung onto the plane's fuselage to keep from falling down. I grabbed the interior frame of the window to keep from falling and used that same grip to pull myself toward the window. After a third explosion, I looked out the window to see black smoke forming a small cloud in midair. It was the German Air Defense anti-aircraft guns firing flak, most likely from German 88s. BOOM! BOOM! BOOM! The flak exploded all around us as the plane continued jumping and quivering. I looked back at Tillins only to see him now on his knees, holding onto the fuselage. He looked at me and all he could say was, "Oh, damn." It only now dawned on me that this ride had been my bad idea and that it could very well be my last!

It was at that very moment the whole formation went into descend mode in preparation for our hedgehop bombing run. I felt the plane's front end tilt hard forward as our pilot followed the lead plane that had also turned its nose hard downward. As we descended, we started drawing substantial ground fire. I remember instinctively jumping every time I heard bullets peppering the hull of the B25. As the plane tilted forward, I looked out the window and couldn't believe how quickly we were dropping in altitude. Our plane was still being jolted with each blast and constantly shaking from the almost continuous explosions of flak surrounding us. Then the airmen on board started to prepare the plane for bombing mode. They opened the bomb bay doors and began preparations to release our payload. I could hear the wind rushing past the open doors, and I could feel the whole plane slow a bit from the wind drag caused by the open bomb bay doors. The further we descended, the more ground fire we started taking.

I looked back at Tillins, only to see him on his hands and knees vomiting on the floor. I don't know if it was just plain fear or if he was suffering from motion sickness. Regardless, he was in awful shape. Next I felt the plane level off just above the treetops. One of the older airmen looked at Tillins and then at me. After staring at me for a second, he said, "Well, son, how do you like this hedgehop bombing?" He laughed and said, "Try not to think about the explosives on board, because if you do, you'll realize this is like flying a stick of dynamite through the gates of hell." Then it dawned on me: this son-of-a-bitch knew how this mission was going to go. By that time, Tillins looked just about ready to die from fear. I was starting to wonder if we were going to live through this, and I had to listen to that older airman making bad jokes at the same time.

All the planes were lined up and on target to drop their bombs in a heavily occupied section of the German frontlines. Somebody hollered, "Okay boys, we're on the final run-in." I watched out the window as the lead B25 dropped its payload. Our planes were crossing the enemy's front line at barely one hundred feet above ground level. The first bombs that fell left nothing but rubble and smoldering ash in places that just seconds before were occupied by enemy troops and equipment. We were flying behind the lead plane by several hundred yards and to its left. Then it was "bombs away" for us as well, and our load was dropped on some existing German structures. When the explosives detonated, the concussion elevated the whole plane and lifted me off my feet as the plane was raised about twenty feet in just a second. When I regained myself, I looked out the window again. I couldn't see the planes behind us, although I could hear the sound of their bombs detonating.

I heard one of the airmen say, "Now it's time to get the hell out of here." At the same time, I could feel our pilot start climbing hard as flak was still exploding all around us. I looked back to check on Tillins, who was now lying spread eagle on the floor. I thought to myself, *Well, at least he won't be falling and getting hurt if he is already on the floor.* I looked out the window. I couldn't believe the amount of fire and smoke we had left on the ground behind us. This mission had definitely been a success; now all we had to do was get back to the airbase in one piece. As we were climbing, we were turning hard to the west. Then I heard and felt the bomb bay doors close and the whole plane speeding quickly up. From the window, I could see that all four of our planes had survived. Flak was still exploding around us, but the worst of it was over. As we headed west, we eventually flew out of range of the flak and were again picked up by our fighter support. Thank God we didn't need them on the return trip, as no enemy planes dared to pursue us.

I sure was relieved when I saw the airport coming up at a distance. I sat Tillins up and wiped his face with a rag. "You're alright, Tillins."

He just looked at me for a while then finally he said, "Those bastards knew what kind of a ride that was going to be."

I said, "I know. You're okay. Don't worry about it. Don't give them the satisfaction by grumbling about it. The hell with them, let's just get off this plane." Tillins just nodded his head, agreeing.

A few minutes later we were coming in for a landing. At the last moment, the plane pitched back and bounced hard as it hit the ground. When the plane came to a stop, the older airman came back to us and asked how we had liked the ride. Tillins answered, "We liked it just fine. It was a really a good ride. Thank you so much. It was great!" Next the airman looked at us and asked if we wanted to go again. I said, "To hell with that! You got to be crazy!" Then out the door we went.

As soon as we were out of earshot, Tillins looked at me and said, "What was that you said about not giving them the satisfaction?"

"I know, I know," I answered.

Then Tillins said, "Well, don't worry about it. I heard one of the gunners saying to another that it was the worst trip he was ever on."

That evening Tillins and I sat and talked with the fellows working at the airfield. When we told them that we were navy guys, we got the same standard response: "What the hell are you guys doing here?" As our conversation went on, we told them all about our hedgehop bombing experience. We emphasized the excitement of the bombing mission and we intentionally left out the parts about how scared to death we really were.

At some point in the story, Tillins leaned over to me and quietly said, "You know, Bill, a fellow could get killed around here!" We both laughed a little and I shook my head. Then we continued explaining our unforgettable experience.

"All these years later as I look back on that flight now, I realize that hitching a ride on that hedgehop bombing run was one of the dumbest things I did during my entire time in the whole war. Nevertheless, I've also always looked back on it as one of the most thrilling and adventurous things I endured during my entire wartime experience. After the war and for the rest of my life, I truly appreciated that experience as one of the finest and most thrilling of my life. After all, it's often the mistakes we make when we're young that create the best memories when we're old. I always get great satisfaction out of remembering taking part in that bombing mission. Looking back, I wouldn't have missed it for the world."

-Bill Grannetino, 1998

Later that evening, we rested. We ate more hot food and got some sleep on padded cots in a heated building. Again, compared to what we were accustomed to, it was like sleeping in a luxury hotel. About midnight we were given a ride back to our truck. When we arrived, the repair crews were finishing up repairing our tires. By 0100, we were back on the road. We immediately drove back to the airbase from which we had just been and unloaded our cargo. After we unloaded, the MPs put us in another convoy heading west, and we started our return trip back to Le Harve.

Over the next few days there was a noticeable change in the weather, as the days were getting colder and colder. We had seen a few snow flurries already and knew that soon we would be dealing with accumulating snow and icy roads. The job certainly wasn't getting any easier; we still never got a real break, and we continued to always be over-tired and worn out. We never got more than a four-hour break in any given week. During those breaks we would shower, change our clothes, eat some hot food, and get some sleep on a cot. Sometimes those breaks were in our tent at La Harve and other times they were at one of the depots to which we delivered.

All of us who were driving trucks were well aware that the further the Allied front pushed east into Germany, the longer and harder our trips would become. The convoy truckers also talked about the fact that the closer our front lines got to Germany, the less distance the Germans' supply convoys would have to cover to supply their troops. The officers who commanded us, the U.S. Army Transport Units, said this fact would give the Germans the advantage of supplying their troops more quickly and easily than we could supply ours. The officers would then always remind us that it was critical that we push harder and harder than ever before to keep our convoys moving nonstop. I'm sure it was easy for all those merciless officers in our Command to say go, go, go around the clock nonstop, because it really didn't affect them the way it affected us. I'm sure they completely took for granted what it meant to get plenty of sleep and hot food on a regular basis. Those unappreciative, worthless sons-a-bitches had no idea what we were going through. To us, those officers were nothing more than ungrateful, thankless, cold-hearted bastards.

Regardless of our resentment, we pushed on and on, day and night, mile after mile. In the first half of December 1944, almost every load we hauled was delivered to the railheads in Paris. Making a round trip from Le Harve to Paris and back again took about eight hours. As I remember, it was sometime in mid-December when Tillins and I were part of a convoy returning to Le Harve from the Paris railheads. Our convoy had pulled over for what was an extremely rare break at a newly constructed roadside tent camp that had been set up as a bivouac area for the truckers running that route. While we were getting some hot coffee and hot food, the cooks told us about a German attack on the American front in Belgium. They referred to this German operation as "the Ardennes counteroffensive." We learned that this battle had already lasted a day or two. We weren't told much more than that. We didn't think too much of it; there were always battles going on somewhere along the American front. Regardless, after an exceptionally long break that lasted about fifty or fifty-five minutes, we got back on the road, again headed to Le Harve.

About three hours later, we were pulling into Le Harve expecting to be reloaded like always, after which we would immediately return to Paris. As we pulled into the harbor front, we could tell there was something strange going on. Men were running everywhere, and there were more trucks being loaded and organized into convoys than we had ever seen there before. When our convoy stopped, officers and MPs hurriedly directed us to get out of our trucks immediately and prepare for a briefing.

They quickly gathered us into a group and we were told to listen up. An MP said, "As we speak, there is a major German counteroffensive going on in the eastern part of Belgium. It's critical that we ship them huge amounts of sorely needed supplies immediately. Because of this unanticipated offensive, we are putting every soldier we can find into our supply trucks—cooks, MPs, clerks, chaplains, mechanics, and every officer we can spare. As you can also see, right now we are gathering every truck we can possibly find and organizing them into convoys that will leave here as quickly as possible. You men aren't going to be waiting for your own trucks to be reloaded; you're going to be leaving right away in other trucks that have already been loaded. You will be driving nonstop into eastern Belgium. There will be no ten-minute breaks. You will not stop for fuel; we will be fueling you on the move. If a truck breaks down, you will not stop, and you will not assist other teams; you are to keep your truck moving at all costs. Now get your gear, get your helmets, and bring your weapons. Waste no time and let's get loaded. We're pulling out immediately."

We were led to a convoy that looked like it was at least a hundred trucks or more that had already been loaded and were ready to go. I was surprised to see how many of the trucks in this convoy were troop carriers that had already been loaded. These fighting men were being sent east to the Ardennes counteroffensive as reinforcements. Tillins and I ended up in a British lorry that was loaded with howitzer artillery shells. Within minutes of being assigned to that new truck, we were on the road headed to Belgium. We started out driving at a steady speed of about forty-five miles per hour. That was a much faster-than-normal speed for a convoy.

The MPs told us we could expect this trip to take twenty to twenty-four hours for a full round trip. Hearing that, Tillins decided to lay back and get some sleep while I started driving. As I remember, that day was very cold with temperatures well below freezing. Our truck was located somewhere in the middle of the convoy. I couldn't see up to the front of the convoy, nor could I see all the way back to the last truck. The roads we were driving on were closed to all traffic except trucks hauling men or supplies to the Ardennes counteroffensive.

After about three hours on the road, I saw a gasoline tanker truck working its way up the side of the convoy. As I watched in my door-mounted rearview mirror, I could see that the fuel truck had the passenger's door tied all the way open with rope. A soldier was standing on the running board behind the open door. This truck pulled up to each supply truck one at a time. They would direct one of the convoy drivers to stand on his truck's running board as the other man drove. When they were in position, the soldier on the fuel truck would throw the convoy driver a fuel line hose with a nozzle on the end. The driver would then fuel his truck without stopping. It was truly an exercise that took some precision timing.

When the fuel truck pulled up next to us, I stepped out onto the running board as Tillins slid into the driver's seat. I immediately removed the gas cap and handed it to Tillins. The soldier on the fuel truck running board yelled, "Are you ready?" I nodded my head yes, and he threw me the hose. I filled the tank with fuel until it started to run over. Then I threw the hose back. He hollered, "How is your oil pressure? If it's a little low, I'll give you a half a quart to dump in."

I said, "No, we're good." With that, he moved up to the next truck. We watched as they filled each fuel tank. Then we watched one of the convoy truck drivers as he swung around the back of the driver's side door. After he had closed the door he stayed outside on the running board. Next, he moved in front of the door's rearview mirror and opened the side hood by unhooking the side straps and pushing the left half of the hood open. I watched the soldier on the fuel truck throw him a quart of oil that he dumped in as they were moving! After adding the oil, he worked his way back into the truck. The fuel truck moved on as they continued down the line.

We drove for what felt like the longest time and saw nothing but roads lined with fence posts on both sides. Closer to the east side of Belgium, the snow was covering the fields and roads. Trucks broke down and others spun around on icy roads, landing in ditches. At times these trucks ended up blocking the road. The convoy escorts and MPs would stop and gather large groups of men to push the trucks out of the way. If the trucks didn't run, they were left behind, along with their drivers. There was no time to worry about a truck that had been left behind. We were always back on the road as quickly as possible and pushing nonstop toward the Ardennes.

After hours of driving at a harder pace than we had ever driven before, we finally pulled into a supply depot near the frontlines. The cargo handling crews were desperately looking for our load of 105MM howitzer shells. They immediately unloaded the shells from our trucks directly into their trucks and then shuttled the ammunition from the depot to the field positions of artillery. These trucks were the same trucks that were used to tow the howitzers from location to location. One of those drivers was telling us how the Germans had been pushing them back, mile after mile. He complained that it took a day or two just to get the commanding officers to believe there was a main counteroffensive launched by an enormous German force, and it wasn't just a small enemy attack. He referred to this fighting as the "Battle of the Bulge" and didn't just refer to it as the Ardennes counteroffensive. This was the first time I heard this engagement called the Battle of the Bulge, but it sure wasn't the last time. As he was leaving he said, "Thank God Eisenhower got off his rear end and is now rushing reinforcements and supplies to the Ardennes before we are all killed."

As soon as we were unloaded, all the trucks in the convoy that didn't already have chains on took the time to wrap chains around their tires so we could traverse more quickly in the snow and ice. Before we pulled out on our return trip, we were warned about German air raids that were targeting truck convoys. It was also decided that on this trip back to Le Harve we would be running empty because there was no time to load and transport anything back to the coast. For the next several days it was around-the-clock shuttling, transporting fuel, supplies and equipment into the Belgian depots. After several continuous days of our efforts, the depots had ample stacks of material.

During December of 1944, the Ardennes had the worst winter weather it had experienced in years, with temperatures falling below 0°F for days at a time. Snow blanketed the small towns, their roads, and deep forests of the area. At this same time, our troops on the frontlines were constantly on the attack and continually having to beat off counterattacks. Mother Nature proved to be as brutal an enemy as the Germans; our men suffered from frozen feet, frostbite, trench foot, battle fatigue, and pneumonia in addition to dealing with the fighting and casualties. Our fellows were exposed to brutal weather day and night—always cold, always hungry, and always frightened.

We continued driving our trucks around-the-clock right through Christmas Day of 1944, as if Christmas didn't even exist. It was sometime between Christmas and New Year's that we again started getting our ten-minute breaks each hour as we had in the past. On one of our return trips to Le Harve, our lieutenant complained that the officer in command was going to kill us if we didn't get a decent break. Soon after that we were given six hours to shower, change clothes, eat, and sleep. A day or two before New Year's, when the inventories of supplies at the Belgian depots were starting to maintain more than adequate stockpiles, we were given a four hour break every time we returned to Le Harve.

I remember New Year's Day 1945. It was still very cold, but on that day the sky finally cleared and the sun started to shine. As I recall, Tillins and I were hauling anti-aircraft shells into the Ardennes. During this trip, I saw the most upsetting things I would see during the Battle of the Bulge. We came to an area where there had been a battle days earlier that left dozens of dead Americans and Germans everywhere. It was easy to tell the difference between the Americans and Germans because the German infantry was wearing white winter camouflage clothing. The dead soldiers from both sides were frozen like rocks and lying in the snow next to dead horses, blown-up trucks, tanks, and equipment. The worst sights were the horrible expressions on their frozen faces, their last expressions before death. Just unspeakable, dreadful-looking, petrified expressions of horror preserved in ice.

The following day when Tillins and I got back to Le Harve, I was told to report to the lieutenant's office immediately. Tillins asked, "What the hell could they want with you?"

"Who knows?" I said. "Listen, Tillins, you go load the truck and I'll find out what they want. Then I'll catch up with you."

To get to the lieutenant's office I had to find a ride back to our tent camp, which was several minutes from the harbor front. I hooked up with one of the MPs I knew and hitched a ride back with him. As soon as I was there, I went right to the lieutenant's office. I told the clerk who I was and that I was told to report. He handed me an envelope, which I immediately opened and read the papers that were inside. It was then that I learned I had new orders. These orders said that I would be on a ship the next morning. It was headed back to the Norfolk Navy Yards in Portsmouth, Virginia. I asked the clerk if he had orders for Seaman Tillins. He looked around and then said, "No. No orders for a Seaman Tillins." *Damn*, I thought, *I have to get back to the harbor before Tillins heads out on his next run.*

I looked around for anyone who could quickly give me a ride back to the harbor. As luck would have it, there was no one headed to the harbor to give me a ride. I decided to head back on foot and then hitch a ride with anyone going in my direction. I left the tent camp running at a moderate pace. I waved down the first truck I saw, jumping onto the running board, and I got a ride to the first intersection. Getting off there, I was back on foot jogging until I got the next ride heading in my direction. Then I got a third ride, followed by another run, and finally onto the fourth and final ride, which took me all the way into the harbor.

I ran down to the harbor's loading area where I found our convoy. It looked as if they had just lined up to get loaded. I walked up to our truck to let Tillins know what was going on. I opened the passenger's door to our truck and there sat a stranger. *Boy*, I thought, *it didn't take long to replace me.* "Hey, Tillins," I hollered.

With that the driver leaned forward and said, "Who?"

Surprised, I responded, "Where is Tillins, the guy that was driving this truck?"

"Oh him, yeah. Well, they said he lost his partner and that he was being teamed up with some other guy who didn't have a partner. That's when they told us to take this truck on account of ours being broke down, ya know."

Now where do I find Tillins? I decided to find our escort to see who they had teamed Tillins up with. A few minutes later I was talking to our escort and found out that Tillins was teamed up with another convoy that was short a driver. I also found out that he was already on his way to Belgium.

Damn, I thought, *I missed Tillins. Damnit, damnit, damnit.* I started walking back to the tent camp. Again I got a couple of rides and did a little walking in between those rides. When I got back to camp, I wrote a note and tied it to Tillins' backpack, giving him my home address and telling him to look me up after the war.

I was standing in that pyramid-shaped tent getting my things together at the Le Harve tent camp when it finally hit me: I was headed to a Navy Yard in Portsmouth, Virginia. I was going back to the States. I was going home. Oh thank God, I was going home. This was great; this was outstanding. I was going home. I didn't have much to pack, and I had until tomorrow morning to get it done. The first thing I was going to do was to sleep and, when I woke up, I was going to shower and change my clothes. I'd eat, pack my bag, and head to the docks to get on a ship heading back to the States.

Later when I had rested, showered, and changed my clothes, I sat down to eat the first meal I had had in months under normal dining conditions! Then I headed back to the tent camp where I grabbed one duffel bag with my personal belongings in it and a second bag with my souvenirs, which included a couple of German rifles, a .45 caliber German luger, and a few other wartime mementoes.

The next morning I was on the dock talking to one of the ship's crew. I made a deal with him about loading my second duffel bag with some of the ship's supplies in exchange for five cartons of cigarettes. We also agreed that for another five cartons of cigarettes he would see that the bag be unloaded at the Navy Yard in Norfolk, Virginia. About three hours after making those arrangements, I was on board ship heading back to the United States.

[CHAPTER 8]

Shipped to the Pacific

We were going to be at sea for several days before our ship would be pulling into Norfolk, Virginia. Believe me, I took full advantage of those days to make up for some of the much needed rest and relaxation that I had missed out on after several months at war. I ate as much good food as I could get while crossing the Atlantic, eating as if every meal was my last. As soon as I disembarked the ship, I had to check in. It was at that time I was informed that I would be given the standard thirty days of military leave after returning from a tour in Europe before being reassigned to my next duty. I first filled out some paperwork and then was set up in temporary military housing for the night. I took my gear to drop it off in my room. Once in the room, I stood there contemplating how I would be spending my first night back in the States. I was trying to remember the last time I had slept in a regular building that had a regular bed with sheets, a blanket, and a pillow covered with a pillowcase. It was going to be a good night.

Later that evening when I was at the chow hall eating dinner, I ran into a fellow from Wilkes-Barre, Pennsylvania, whose family was picking him up the next day. He offered me a ride and said he could have his dad drop me off along the way at my home in Bath, Pennsylvania. I gladly accepted. The following morning, I headed down to the dock and paid five more cartons of cigarettes to pick up my duffel bag of souvenirs. By midmorning I was homeward bound for the first time in well over a year.

It was only a few hours later that I was dropped off at my home. Stepping out of the car and looking at the house I grew up in, I was hit by all kinds of thoughts, from enthusiasm to just plain satisfaction. Having known only the madness of war for the past year, it was hard to believe I had made it back. I now would be home for thirty days to rest and relax before I had to return to one of those naval bases somewhere around Norfolk, Virginia. It was good to be back and great to see my father, my youngest brother Lou and my little sister Rose. My dad welcomed me home by cooking me lots of fried potatoes for dinner as several neighbors stopped in to visit. They all had questions about where I was and what I did in France. Somehow I avoided answering those questions; it would be years until I was ready to dig up those daunting memories.

The next morning I gathered as much information as I could to locate my brother Henry, who was serving his own navy assignments. After reading the couple of letters he had sent home and talking to some of his friends, I made an educated guess that he was somewhere in the south Pacific. After I was satisfied that I had as much information as I was going to get, I decided to put my duffel bag of souvenirs in a safe place in the garage. I opened up the garage and stashed my things in the garage's attic space.

Next I decided to uncover my Indian motorcycle. I figured I would start the engine to run it, knowing it hadn't been started for at least two years. Now it was January, so it was very cold outside. Between the cold, old gas, and the engine not having been run in a long time, it took me a while and a little work to get it started. Finally I got it to fire up. The thunderous roar of the engine brought back memories I had long forgotten. I opened the garage door, pulled that old Indian out into the snowy alley, and drove it back and forth a few times. Although I was only moving slowly, I was freezing. After two or three laps, I quickly pulled back into the garage, parked the bike, and covered it up. Then I hurried back into the house and stood on top of the floor grate in our living room, which was mounted over our basement coal furnace.

While I was warming up, the phone rang. My dad answered it. In his broken Italian accent, I could hear him asking the person on the other end who they were and who they wanted. As he went back and forth on the phone, I heard him say, "Navy." Next, I heard him say, "Billy."

With that, I took the phone and said, "This is Bill Grannetino. Who is this?" The fellow on the other end of the phone said he was a clerk in a Norfolk, Virginia, navy personnel office. He explained that he was calling to inform me that my leave was being canceled and I was being recalled to active duty immediately. He asked if I could be back within forty-eight hours! My attitude changed in a split second and I wasn't too happy. In a not-so-polite tone, I said to the clerk, "Hell no, there's no goddamn way I'm coming back in forty-eight hours. This has to be a mistake. I have thirty days of leave coming, and I'm not giving them up. I did my duty in Europe for the last several months. I put my ass on the line more than once. This *has* to be a mistake. You go back to whoever gave you these orders and tell them Bill Grannetino will see you in thirty days."

In a stuttering, reluctant voice he said okay and that, yes, he would check it out and get back to me if it wasn't a mistake. After I hung up the phone without saying goodbye, I had to explain to my dad what was going on.

I spent the rest of my day visiting old friends down at the filling station where I had worked as a kid. I spent most of my time talking to the older World War I vets about the war in Europe and what we still had coming in Japan.

When I got home, my dad was cleaning more potatoes and some squash for dinner. He said that the clerk from that navy personnel office had called back and left a number for me to call him back.

"The hell with him," I said. "I'm not calling him back. If they think I'm giving up my thirty days leave, they're crazy." Later that evening Dad and I were listening to the news about the war on the radio when the phone rang again. I wasn't paying too much attention, as I was trying to hear what was happening overseas. Next thing I know, Dad's handing me the phone and telling me it's that "navy fellow" for the third time. *Damn*, I was thinking as I reluctantly took the phone. Yep, it was that damn navy clerk again. He asked that I confirm that he was speaking to William Grannetino. I did and asked what he wanted now. He explained that he completely and thoroughly reviewed the canceling of my leave and he wanted to reassure me that it was not a mistake. He said I had forty-eight hours to return or

I would be considered AWOL. "Listen," I said, "you go back and tell those sons-a-bitches that I have thirty days of leave coming and that I'm taking them! You also let them know that I'm just one man in the whole United States Navy. There's no way they can't just find some other son-of-a-bitch to do whatever it is they want me to do. Now listen to me, mister, and do us both a favor—don't call me again and I'll see you folks in thirty days."

Then the clerk said in a very meek and submissive voice, "Well, I'm going to have to report this to the higher-ups and I'm not going to be responsible for the outcome if you choose to ignore this request."

I said, "That's just fine! Don't bother calling back! Goodbye." I angrily hung up the phone.

I spent most of the next day visiting a few high school friends. Unfortunately, most of the fellows I grew up with were in the military on active duty. On the other hand, there were several young ladies with whom I could share a leisurely day! I truly had an excellent day talking, visiting, and flirting with the girls. I even invited one of the young ladies home to have dinner at my house. We ate, spent time listening to the radio, talked, laughed, and I spent a fair amount of time flirting. It had been so long since I had gotten to charm a young lady, I was surprised I even remembered how to flirt with a cute girl! At the end of the evening, sometime around midnight, I walked her home. As we walked, we made plans to meet for lunch the next day at the local restaurant. As I was returning home, I was somewhat taken aback by the real satisfaction I felt from all this normal social interaction and just how great it felt to be home.

The next morning I woke up late. My dad was already at work and my younger sister and brother were both in school. I was in the kitchen getting something to eat when I heard a knock on the front door. I went to the large window in the living room and looked out to see who it was. *Damn.* There were two really big fellows in Navy uniforms standing on our front porch. This had to be about my returning early. *Well,* I thought, *there is no getting around this; I had better answer the door.*

As I opened the door, one of the men immediately said, "Are you William Grannetino?" I nodded my head and said "Yes." He then asked if they could come in and talk with me. I opened the door and said, "Sure. Come in." As soon as we were in the living room, they introduced themselves and said they were Navy Military police officers. One of them said I should relax, that they weren't there to arrest me, but rather to help me. He went on to explain that they were aware of my training and my service overseas. He mentioned Omaha, he knew about the time I had spent with the British and finally my duty based out of La Harve. He said that the citizens of the United States definitely owed me recognition and their appreciation for the honorable service I had loyally performed for our country. He explained that the navy had given my service great consideration, and that it was with this service in mind that they were going to give me a second chance to immediately return to active duty as requested.

I told them that I felt I should get thirty days of leave just like everybody else who returned from Europe. I said, "I could have been killed on more than one occasion. Besides that, I can't imagine I'm the only fellow in this whole navy that can do whatever I'm being assigned to do." I finished by saying, "What's fair is fair."

He replied, "Orders are orders."

"What are your intentions?" I asked. "What happens if I say I'm not coming back until my thirty days are up?"

He answered, "Please understand this ... we're taking you back with us one way or another. Either you get in the car and go with us willingly, or like it or not, we're going to put you into the car and take you back with us."

Reluctantly, I realized I had to accept my fate. I asked how long I had to get my things together. With that, the MP smiled and said, "Thank you for making the right decision; take as long as you need." Within a few minutes, I had changed my clothes and packed my personal things.

"One more thing," I said. "I need to tell my neighbor that I have to return to active duty early so he can explain it to my dad when he gets home from work this evening. I can't leave my dad a note. He doesn't read or write." After I finished explaining my situation to the neighbor, I also asked him to let the young lady I was intending to have lunch with know that I was being recalled to active duty.

As soon as the two Navy policemen and I were on the road headed to Norfolk, they started asking me questions about the war in Europe. They were especially interested in the landings on D-Day. We talked for about two hours before one of them said it was time to pull over and get a little lunch. We went into a small diner for a couple of burgers. and continued talking about the war for another hour or so before getting back on the road. They turned out to be really nice fellows. For them, "ignorance was bliss" (no disrespect intended), for they had no idea what war was really like, except for the stories that they heard on the radio or read in the newspaper. To say the least, they were so "wet behind the ears," they believed being in action was a righteous thing—a coming-of-age experience for all young men. They had no idea how horrible war really was or how terrible seeing death could be. Most of all, they had no idea how terrifying real fear was, when bullets filled the air around you and any breath you took could be your last. I didn't even try to tell them the truth. I just listened to them go on and on about how they wished they could see some action. They just kept talking about how they were stuck here in the States and how they would rather be fighting overseas. Sure, they were nice fellows, but to me it was laughable how naive they really were. They didn't have any idea how good they really had it. I would have traded places with them in a heartbeat.

Later that evening, the Navy policemen dropped me off at the Norfolk Navy Yard in Portsmouth, Virginia. You would think we were family by the way they said goodbye and were wishing me well. If I had been forced to spend another hour with those fellows, I think it would have killed me. I reported in and, thankfully, not a word was said about my not showing up on time. The officer I reported to told me that I was going to be assigned to a ship that was setting sail in the morning. He directed me to a fleet tug called the USS *Endure*. After I was on board, I was told that small tugs like these were the workhorses of the fleet. These tugs were used for towing, diving operations, minesweeping, salvage undertakings, distilling fresh water for other ships, and rescuing ships that for any reason had lost power. With its four diesel engines running electric generators, this ship could develop three thousand horse power from the electric motors turning its fifteen-foot screws to tow the largest of vessels or dry-dock sections for long distances at sea.

The *Endure* had recently returned from its shakedown cruise, otherwise known as a test run. After the shakedown trials in the Chesapeake Bay, the tug reported to the Norfolk Navy Yard for post-shakedown repairs. Some of the "bugs" in running the ship had to be worked out while in the yard. Adjustments had been made to suit the crew and the captain. Just as I arrived, the ship was scheduled to leave the next day for emergency duty. Then I understood why I had lost my leave. Turns out the *Endure* was being ordered to immediately proceed to the Hudson River, which had frozen over to a depth of two to three feet. It was planned that *Endure* would clear a path to Iona Island so ammunition barges could be moved down the river. It would have started its next assignment a month later if the winter weather had been just a few degrees warmer. Even though the *Endure* wasn't designed as an icebreaker, it was built with a very heavy steel hull, and with its enormous engine power would be able to clear a path up to Long Island so that ammunition barges could be moved down the river.

Turns out the New York City duty was an excellent assignment and a very safe duty as compared to the sailors serving in the Atlantic or the Pacific. On top of that, there was another benefit of being in New York City: on a couple of evenings we had a chance to get off the ship and tour the "Big Apple." I was amazed at the nightlife in the city; places like jazz music joints, dancing halls, bars with entertainment and the modern movie houses thrilled me. Being raised in a small town, I had never seen a city breathe so much life into the night. Noisy traffic, crowded streets, sleazy bars, dirty subways, outlandish people, and the overall urban environment was unbelievably exciting! It was also somewhat intimidating and, in some ways, overwhelmed me. After a couple of weeks of this duty, I was hoping I would get to serve the rest of my remaining navy time protecting the eastern coast of the United States, or the "American Theater" as the military called it at the time.

On an average winter day, we would run up river, breaking ice as we went. The tug would easily run through ice a foot or so thick. When the ice was two or three feet thick, the tug would slide up the ice until it collapsed under the ship's weight. During this time, I became very familiar with the engine room as well as the running of the engines themselves. I learned their weakness as well as their strengths. It was a great lesson that I would use all through my time serving in the Pacific.

The *Endure* wa had been pretty safe and in many ways was turning out to be interesting and educational. I was working with some really good fellows overall s also set up with large distillers to make considerable quantities of fresh water to be delivered to other ships. During this preliminary voyage, I started making fresh water and getting familiar with all the various engine room operations.

Sometime in the beginning of March, 1945, the New York City assignment was finished and we returned to Norfolk for a short time before sailing to New Orleans. In New Orleans, we picked up a large barge and pulled it into Gulfport, Mississippi, where it was loaded with ammunition. We then departed from Mississippi sometime in late March, heading for the Pacific. We first sailed south to the Panama Canal. After passing through the canal, we towed our ammunition barge west to Hawaii, where we were to offload a portion of our cargo and be refueled.

The crew was looking forward to seeing the remnants of the attack on Pearl Harbor. It had been over three years since that famous attack brought the United States into the war. As we were approaching Pearl, we were contacted and told to stop five miles out at sea and not to enter the harbor. A message was sent out to us saying that because we were towing ammunitions, we could be jeopardizing the safety of the harbor, and that a barge would be brought out to us to offload Pearl's portion of the cargo. You cannot imagine how disappointed the crew was over that news.

The next morning a fleet tug, very similar to ours, towed a barge out to us that was then used to transport their allocation of our load into the harbor. A second barge, a floating fuel barge, later carried fuel to us. After refueling, we headed south for Bora Bora.

As we approached Bora Bora, we saw what looked like one giant mountain peak surrounded by several small islands. Bora Bora was a smaller group of islands. The lagoon was huge in comparison to the amount of land mass around it. Its waters appeared transparent over the white sand on the ocean floor. I was amazed at the range of shades of blue and turquoise water. After we navigated into the waters of the lagoon, we were directed to anchor our tug and wait to have the barge we were towing picked up by a couple of smaller tugs. Those tugs then pushed the cargo we delivered into the harbor docks to be unloaded. As we waited, we could see manta rays and sharks swimming in the clear waters of the lagoon. Its beauty made it hard to believe this place was a military supply base, fuel oil depot, and defensive fortification.

After we delivered our cargo, we docked for refueling. When our tug was secured and the gangplank was down, we were given some free time off the ship. For a twenty-one-year-old kid who had never seen a tropical island before, the place was unbelievable. I was fascinated by the palm trees as well as many of the other exotic plants and flowers. The white sand beaches and the volcanic rock formations were also incredible. I remember walking through villages with grass huts and seeing how the local people lived. While there, I ate some of the local foods and tasted their homemade alcoholic drinks. I remember taking in all these new experiences and, once again, felt pretty lucky for a kid from small-town America.

The following day our captain was told that the supply barge we were scheduled to tow to the next port wouldn't be ready for another day or so. That being the case, we had time to do some more touring around the island. One of the navy fellows working on the docks said we should go to an observation point along the coast on the inside of the lagoons and watch the seaplanes landing and taking off from the seaport. Since none of us had ever even seen a seaplane before, we made our way to the observation point and spent hours watching several seaplanes taking off and landing.

You have to realize that as kids raised in the 1930s, we were yet at a time in history when air travel had become commonplace. During those years, if my brothers and my sister even heard a plane flying over our town, we and our entire neighborhood would run outside just to get a look at it. To us, watching those planes was something pretty amazing and awe-inspiring.

-Bill Grannetino, 1998

The next day we left Bora Bora towing another supply barge heading west to New Guinea. That was the beginning of a month or two of carrying out a variety of towing operations among the Philippine Islands, Indonesia, Australia, New Zealand, and New Guinea. We towed barges filled with weapons, ammunition, supplies, fuel, and just about anything else you could imagine. We towed ships with mechanical problems back to port for repairs. On a few occasions, we even towed ships that had been disabled in battle. In combination with our towing operations, we were constantly running our distillers and making fresh water that we would deliver to various other larger ships. This was a very busy time; rarely did we get an opportunity to tour as we had in Bora Bora.

It was during this time that we got the news that Hitler was dead and the war in Europe was over. On board ship, there was a lot of talk about how much longer it would take to end this war against the Japanese in the Pacific. I think the overall consensus was at least two more years.

Our duty in the Pacific so far had been pretty safe and in many ways was turning out to be interesting and educational. I was working with some really good fellows overall. The *Endure* had a small crew of sixty-eight men, so we all got to know each other fairly well. Regardless of getting to know all those new guys, I sure missed my good friend Tillins. I often wondered where Tillins was serving now and how he was doing. Was he on a ship in the Atlantic, or was he somewhere in the Pacific? Could he be back in the States by now? Who knew? Nevertheless, he was often on my mind. Be that as it may, I truly did enjoy the camaraderie I found with my new crewmates. We had lots of good times while serving on the *Endure*. I especially enjoyed watching the guys when they had a chance to do some fishing over the side of the ship. Every time we stopped for any reason, several crewmen would take advantage of that time to do some fishing. We didn't have fishing poles or tackle on board for fishing, but bored crewmen are nothing if not innovative. These fellows used hand lines made of twine; others used pipes as poles with wire for line. Some used electric wire tied to a short piece of wood. Hooks were made from spring steel that had been hand-filed into shape for fishing.

When these fellows caught fish for the first time off the side of the ship, they cleaned them and proceeded to carry them into the galley to be cooked. Apparently, the chief cook didn't take kindly to just anyone bringing fish into his kitchen. As quickly as they went into the galley, they came right back out, still carrying their fish. Next thing you know, these fellows came to see me in the engine room, wanting to know if they could cook the fish on the engines. We cleaned a tool tray really well with soap and water. Then we put the fish into the tray and laid it on the engines to cook. An hour later, we were eating some of the best fish I had ever eaten in my life. We had fish like this many times during my time on the *Endure.* As time went on, we stocked up on cooking oil, butter, and spices to improve our engine-room cooking.

Ever since we started carrying out our many towing operations in the South Pacific, we had been hearing bits and pieces about different U.S. ships and how they were being sunk. We heard some ships had been torpedoed by submarines while others were devastated by the huge guns of the Japanese battleships. Still others were bombed from enemy aircraft or they sank when they struck a mine. All those things were terrifying in their own way, but not nearly as intimidating as the stories we heard about ships being struck by a kamikaze.

It was around that time that we reached the waters of the East China Sea near Japan. We were then performing our towing duties in the area of Okinawa and many of the islands that surrounded it. By that time, the battle for Okinawa had already been going on for several weeks. For us, this was the first time we were near hostile activity in the Pacific or close to an area where there were regular kamikaze attacks.

As we were carrying out our towing operations and traveling from port to port, we learned that at least twenty ships around Okinawa had already been sunk one way or another during the Battle of Okinawa. Most of the lost ships were struck by kamikazes, a few hit mines, and some were shelled or attacked by regular Japanese aircraft. By the time we arrived, there were at least ten more ships damaged or sunk in the area. Everybody on board was concerned about the possibility of a kamikaze attack on our ship.

Late one night when we were hauling ammunitions toward a supply depot near Okinawa, I was down in the ship's engine room when there was a huge commotion. I saw several fellows scrambling up onto the deck. As soon as I could break free from my duties, I went up to see what was going on. From a distance, I could see the sky lit up by tracers being shot into the air from a team of U.S. ships a couple of miles away from us performing picket duty off the coast of Okinawa. "What's going on?" I asked. "What are they shooting at?" One of our fellows said he thought they were being attacked by kamikazes. As far away as we were, we could only hear a little of the sound of gunfire and flak and really couldn't see what was going on. We watched for a few minutes, and then we were told to return to our posts. As soon as I was back down in the engine room, I was ordered to run the engines at full speed as we exited the area in full blackout mode. Since we were towing ammunitions, that order made good sense and was understood by all. I certainly wasn't going to complain—the further away we were from the Okinawa action, the better.

The next day when we were delivering our cargo, it was confirmed that it was a kamikaze attack that we had seen from a distance. From what we heard, the ships that had been targeted had shot down all the attacking planes. No U.S. ships had been hit. When we were talking to our captain about kamikaze attacks, he said we shouldn't worry about it all that much, *that only one out of seven kamikaze attacks sank ships outright.* That was still a percentage I wasn't too happy with and one I certainly wouldn't be willing to risk given the choice. I don't think anyone appreciated the captain's sarcasm.

It wasn't long after this that we got the call to tow a ship that had been devastated by kamikazes and several other attacking Japanese planes during the Battle of Okinawa. We were directed to pick up and tow a huge floating dry-dock to a small island west of Okinawa. There we loaded a severely damaged battleship into the dry-dock so it could be taken to a better-equipped naval base for repairs. There they would have the ability to provide repairs that were more extensive. When I saw the extent of the damage caused by the attack, I couldn't believe the ship didn't sink, as it resembled a hunk of twisted and mangled steel more than anything else. It had been hit by two or three kamikazes, completely mutilating its upper decks into several large sections of damage. I could see where the fires had followed those explosions, doing equally as much damage as the impact. Metal was melted and bent as if it was plastic that had gotten so hot it had become soft and pliable. Complete sections of decks were gone. Below the waterline, the ship had a large, gaping hole in its side, along with countless small holes, the totality of which flooded several sections of the hull. In the rear, the propellers were damaged from bombs that must have fallen just behind the ship. Seeing that ship scared all of us as we witnessed firsthand how devastating a kamikaze attack could be. After the ship was loaded into the dry-dock, we towed it fifty or sixty miles to a large bay on the east side of Okinawa. We called it Buckner Bay. I can't begin to imagine how many sailors must have died on that ship.

At about this time, the Battle of Okinawa was ending, thank God. It was also during this time in the Pacific war that many ships in the area of Okinawa, including ours, were primarily stationed at Buckner Bay. Buckner Bay was becoming a main command center for that region's naval operations. For the immediate future, the *Endure* would remain there performing routine towing and fuel re-supply operations, and making and providing distilled water to other warships.

After a few weeks of working on these duties, our captain received orders to have our tug converted into a minesweeping ship. We were then informed that our role as a minesweeper would be to enter Japanese-defended waters and clear lanes through ocean minefields. By doing so, the planned invasion fleet could get to the shores of Japan to land our troops for the impending land assault. We all realized being on a minesweeper ahead of the approaching landings meant we would become the main target of the kamikazes. We might as well have painted a huge red target circle on our deck.

While we were docked in Buckner Bay during the time our tug was being converted for minesweeping operations, another ship in our area was struck and sunk by a lone kamikaze. A single kamikaze pilot had made his way past Buckner's perimeter defenses and attacked an area where several of our ships were moored. At that point in our deployment, we were becoming used to hearing about regular kamikaze attacks. It seemed every day or two since we had arrived in the area of Okinawa a ship was sunk or damaged by a kamikaze attack somewhere around the islands. Now that we were scheduled to sweep mines off the coast of Japan in preparation for the invasion fleet, we were much more sensitive about these reports. Actually, to tell you the truth, some fellows shook with outright fear when we talked about our upcoming duties. All I could think about was the fact that we would be clearing the way for another D-Day invasion. God forbid I would be reassigned to another LCT for an invasion of Japan. Going unscathed through hell once was enough for me, I wasn't eager to test my luck a second time.

After the new minesweeping gear had been mounted on the ship, we received classroom instructions on how to operate the new equipment. Following that, we sailed out into the open ocean and practiced with other minesweepers, running our new gear through the water in unison. Our fleet of minesweepers working in unison swept a five-mile wide section of ocean in a single pass by lining up minesweeper to minesweeper, with each one traveling in its own lane a half mile ahead of the other. Each minesweeper had a cable attached to a paravane that was extended out to the side of the ship about 3/4 of a mile. A paravane was a torpedo-shaped device with saw-like teeth on the front end. The paravane was towed on the end of a metal cable underwater, stretching from the ship to cut the cables of moored mines up to 3/4 of a mile off the side of our minesweeping ships. This cutting of the mooring cables caused the mines to rise to the surface, then at a safe distance, the mines could be detonated by machine gun fire hitting one of the many detonators sticking out of the mine. Also assisting with cutting the cable were "otters," additional specialized devices with serrated teeth to also cut the mine's attachment lines to the seafloor.

While we were running these practice maneuvers, we heard the news about the atom bomb being dropped on Hiroshima. For the rest of that day and the following day, our radioman gathered every bit of information he could. Every time he got another small piece of information, it spread around the ship like wildfire. We anxiously awaited more information. We heard that 100,000 people died and a whole city was leveled by one bomb. Finally, after two days, our radioman communicated with another radioman somewhere near the Philippines. Apparently this fellow had received information from someone who had read a British newspaper. After he verified the information, we all gathered for an update.

You could have heard a pin drop when he started to read from his notes: President Harry S. Truman informed Americans that an atom bomb was dropped on Hiroshima; a bomb that was more powerful than twenty thousand tons of T.N.T. and that was two thousand times more powerful than the largest bomb ever used in the history of warfare. Truman said the Japanese started this war at Pearl Harbor; now they got what was coming to them and this wasn't over yet. Now that America had harnessed the power of the universe, Truman claimed we were ready to obliterate the Japanese industrial ability to supply their military. Now it is to be the plan of America to destroy every dock, every factory, and all communications in Japan. Truman said, Let there be no mistake; we shall completely destroy Japan's power to make war.

In retrospect, it was clear he meant business.

We were all thrilled to hear about the strength of America. We talked about the atom bomb and about how strong the words of Truman were. Many of the sailors were saying things like, "I hope they drop fifty atom bombs on the Japs and kill every one of the yellow bastards." War hadn't changed my basically pacifist nature; however, I did hope that the bombs were a means to an end, a path to an earlier end, so I could get home as soon as possible.

A few days after this, we heard there was a second bomb dropped on Nagasaki. It again took a day or two, but we finally got some information about the second bomb. The radioman told us President Truman had made another statement. In this announcement, he reported the first atomic bomb was dropped on Hiroshima, a strong military area. He then acknowledged Nagasaki was a manufacturing area and some 75,000 people had died. Truman said this was only a warning of the horrible things to come. Again the crew was all pumped up over the power of America and that we had again slammed the dreadful Japanese.

We couldn't help but wonder how many more atom bombs would be dropped on Japan before the war would end. The Japanese were a resilient, proud folk, and it would take a lot to discourage them from not continuing with the war. That said, we were sure hoping the Japanese would surrender soon, because none of us wanted to be part of any land invasion of Japan.

It was around this time that we completed our minesweeper training and were assigned to a task force under the command of Captain H. J. Armstrong. We cruised out of Buckner Bay with about fifty other minesweepers and various other support ships, as we were assigned to the East China Sea for minesweeping duties.

The first day of minesweeping went like clockwork. Our group of sweepers lined up in their lanes and started sweeping and cutting mines loose from the sea floor. I found it amazing to watch as the wings of the paravane forced the device's body away from the side of our ship and placed lateral tension on the towing cable. When the tow cable snagged the first mooring cable anchored to a mine, the anchoring cable was easily cut and up came the mine, floating to the surface. As soon as it was on the surface and at a safe distance from our ship, it was quickly destroyed in a huge explosion by machine gun fire from the deck of our ship. It was an amazingly efficient operation to observe.

I believe it was on our second day of sweeping that a couple of crewmen on another ship saw a Japanese plane at a distance. All the ships in our flotilla were put on full alert. Fear of a kamikaze attack immediately ran through everybody. We went to battle stations as the plane circled our group of ships at a great distance. Would there be more planes coming? Was this a kamikaze or an attack of fighters and torpedo planes? The minesweeping cables were pulled in as we waited to see what was going to happen.

Even though this Japanese plane was well out of range, one of the ships on the outside of our task force opened up with machine gun fire, sending tracers into the sky. With that, the Jap pilot quickly turned and hightailed it out of there. We expected to see more planes at any minute. We waited at our battle stations for hours. Nothing … not a thing. Finally we got the orders: all clear; return to your minesweeping duties.

It didn't take long before we were back in full operation, cutting mines free and destroying them with machine gun fire. For the next several days, we worked our regular navy shift of four hours on and four hours off. On some of my time off-duty, I would take my daily rum ration and just stand on deck watching this huge undertaking. Ships lined up for miles, each in its own sweeping lane. As I looked out across the ocean, I could see several uniform lines of ships and their wakes streaming behind the minesweepers.

Intermittently there would be the sound of machine gun fire, shortly followed by the explosion of a mine. Sometimes the sounds were far off; some of the sounds came from the ships near us and, for sure, there was no mistaking when it was the *Endure* destroying a surfaced mine.

After we had been in full operation for about a week, and at a time when I was down in the engine room running the distillers, I heard screaming and hollering up on deck. Before I could react, a crewman came running into the engine room. "The war is over! The war is over! The Japs surrendered, Bill! It's over! The war is over!" I went up on deck and saw the crew celebrating, laughing, and carrying on.

The captain was in with the radioman getting confirmation on the information. I was thinking to myself, *God, I hope this is true*. After a few minutes, the captain came out and confirmed the Japanese had surrendered. He then added, "Don't get too comfortable. There are still lots of Japs out there that didn't hear this news yet. That means we are still targets and could be attacked by a sub or a plane at any time. Also, keep this in mind: We still need to finish the job we started. Whether the war is over or not, these mines still need to be cleared. Let's get back to our duties and stay alert."

It took another week or so to complete the sweeping of mines in our zone. By the time we had given this area of ocean the all-clear, our entire task group had swept nearly six hundred total mines during a two-week operation. We saw no real enemy action during the entire operation, but we had learned of some great news. The Japanese had surrendered. As we steamed back to Buckner Bay, all we could talk about was going home. The whole crew was truly thankful that now there would be no need for an invasion of Japan. That invasion would have been a hundred times more awful than the invasion of Okinawa, which was absolutely horrible.

When the *Endure* was through sweeping mines and had returned to Buckner Bay, our ship was immediately reassigned to perform routine towing operations, refueling assignments, a few transport duties, and, as always, provide distilled water to other ships. There was lots of talk on board about the war ending. It sure seemed that truly solid information about what was going on in the war was hard to come by. Being on the ocean the majority of our time just about completely isolated us from current news reports. We were constantly asking the radioman if he had received any new information.

After a week or two, the *Endure* was ordered to leave Buckner Bay and head toward Japan with a few other ships, creating a small task force. When we had reached the southern end of Japan just outside the city of Sasebo, we sat about ten miles offshore and waited for further instructions. During this time, we got the news that General MacArthur had signed the instrument of surrender in Tokyo. The war was now officially over.

After a few more days of waiting, we were finally directed to an area outside the Sasebo Harbor where there were Japanese minefields that would need sweeping. We immediately started making sweeping runs back and forth, starting about five miles off the coast of Japan. It took a little more than a week and a half to cut all the mines free and destroy them. It was the *Endure* that totally cleared the minefields in this area. I would estimate we detonated about fifty mines.

When we were finished with these minesweeping duties, we rejoined the small task force we had sailed with to Sasebo. Next we were told to prepare to enter the harbor at Sasebo. It was at this time I was told that I would be assigned to shore duty in Sasebo Harbor for the next several months. I would be in charge of several crews of sailors who would be dismantling the Japanese shipyards.

I would sure miss that ship; for me, serving on the USS Endure was a really great experience. I had made the rank of Chief Petty Officer on this ship while serving as Chief of the engine room. I was responsible for running the engines. I'll always remember how much I enjoyed rebuilding those engines while underway. I also enjoy the memory of being in charge of maintaining all the mechanical systems on board the ship. There is a particular pride I feel when recalling how I operated the distillers onboard the Endure. It was unbelievable how much fresh water I distilled and supplied to other ships. Making fresh water is an art in its own right. I think back on things like pulling the dry-docks, sweeping for mines, salvage jobs, and towing ships. They were all great experiences that I used and built on throughout my life. I look back on it now and have to say that my mechanical abilities and overall success in life were based on much of this time in the navy.

-Bill Grannetino, 1998

The *Endure* was among the first American ships chosen to sail into Sasebo Bay. The next mission for us as Americans would be to keep Truman's promise and make sure Japan would no longer have the power to make war. As we slowly sailed into the harbor, we were concerned about some sort of attacks from a rogue group of Japanese soldiers. The Japanese had been directed to drape tarps or canvas over the barrels of their shore batteries located at the sides of the entrance to Sasebo Bay. This was done to indicate they wouldn't fire on us. Our task force was told not to shoot at them if they were covered. Likewise, if they were not covered, then our battleships were to fire on them. Thank God all the Japanese guns were covered.

Lots of fishing boats were anchored just outside the main harbor. It only took a minute to see that the Imperial Navy shipyard was built in the area of an old and aging fishing village. The association between the shipyard and the surrounding fishing village was stark. This deep-water harbor was surrounded by mountains and had hundreds of islands off the shorelines throughout the entire bay. It included a major shipyard and had a complete naval repair facility.

After we watched several other ships entering the harbor, it was finally our turn to proceed into the Imperial shipyards. As the *Endure* entered the harbor, I could see some of what was left of the Japanese Navy. I was thoroughly amazed as I looked at Japanese battleships, destroyers, cruisers, and even subs anchored in the harbor just sitting there tranquilly. I didn't see a single man standing on one of their decks. At the direction of the Japanese harbormaster, our ships slowly and gingerly navigated into the harbor. We serenely sailed right past those anchored ships of war to docks that had been designated for the American-occupying ships.

A few ships pulled up to and tied off at docks, while several others, including the *Endure*, anchored in the harbor. I was standing on the deck as I watched American soldiers unload and begin occupying the entire naval facility. It was at that time the captain walked up to me and said, "Chief, it's time for you to report for shore duty. As I had told you before, you will be helping with the disarmament of this naval facility. I recommended you as a man who could lead other men and get the job done. You are still a crewmember of the *Endure*, but for the next few months, you will be on this shore duty. I want to thank you for your service onboard the *Endure* over the last few months. I appreciate the job you did while you were in charge of the engine room. Thank you and good luck. I know you will do well." With that, I collected all my personal gear and within a few minutes was on a small shuttle boat headed to shore.

As soon as I was on shore, I was directed to an office with three other chiefs, guys like myself that were handpicked for this duty. The four of us were briefed by a navy lieutenant. He laid out a blueprint of the entire Japanese facility and designated four areas to be dismantled. I was assigned to oversee the disassembly of the repair facility. The lieutenant explained that the next morning we would each receive crews of sailors, tools, torches, and all the equipment we needed to undertake this job. Along with all the American equipment we had coming, we would also be utilizing the Japanese cranes, forklifts, and any of the equipment and tools already at the facility. It was then suggested that we go and walk our assigned areas and prepare a preliminary plan for our upcoming duties.

Minutes later, I was walking into the repair facility. Inside I saw there were a couple of soldiers who had been assigned to guard duty of this facility. As I looked across the facility, I couldn't believe how huge and cavernous it was. It had cranes, machinery, trucks, and all kinds of heavy equipment parked in rows that seemed to stretch on forever, all of which were to be removed. I walked through welding shops, metal working shops, and electrical, plumbing and carpenter shops. I started making plans as to where I would start my crews the next day, knowing full well this would be no quick or easy task.

After seeing most of the shops, I walked into an office area where I had planned to set up a place for a couple of clerks to do paperwork and keep records of our operation. As soon as I walked through the door, I got the unsettling feeling that someone was watching me. Immediately I noticed movement to my side. I turned, looked, and was stunned for a moment as I realized a Japanese officer was standing about fifteen feet from me. I turned and looked at him. He was wearing a full white uniform, white shoes, white gloves, and he had on a white hat with a black brim. His white jacket was closed with large, gold buttons and it had a collar that stood straight up and wrapped completely around his neck. His uniform had large shoulder panels on it, and the left side of his chest was covered with battle strips.

There wasn't a single speck of dirt or dust on his pristine uniform. He was standing at attention. I noticed he was holding a sword in his left hand that was still in its metal sheath. At that moment, he bowed his head, stuck both arms out in front of himself with both palms turned up as he shifted the sword into each hand and presented it to me. I was astonished and somewhat amazed. I took the sword without saying a word, knowing full well he wouldn't understand me even if I had been able to speak at that moment. The Japanese officer then looked me in the eye and said something in Japanese. He bowed again, turned, and walked away.

As soon as he was gone, I quickly went out to the soldiers guarding the facility and told them there was a Japanese officer still in the office. They said, that yes of course they knew, and he was the officer who ran this facility. The plan was to keep him around for information that might help us with the dismantling. One of the guards then added, "If you need to talk to him, we can get the interpreter back. He left just before you got here. The Japanese officer was told that you wouldn't need him until tomorrow after you started your demolition operation."

I just nodded my head and stood quietly thinking about what had just taken place. Then one of the guards said, "Nice souvenir you got there. You're lucky I didn't find it first." I just smiled a little and agreeably said, "Ya, yes, it is, a nice souvenir."

"All these years later, I still have that sword, and it remains one of my most prized possessions."

-Bill Grannetino, 1998

I spent that night on an American Liberty ship that was docked at the repair facility for the crews doing the demolition work. The next morning I was up early and started organizing crews of sailors in different sections as the demolition operations began. It didn't take me long to realize that the operation would take months.

After a week or so on the job, someone arranged for local Japanese women to bring lunch in for the work crews. The food was unbelievable. I had no idea what kind of Japanese food we were eating, but it sure was the best food I'd eaten in months. For the work crews, lunch became the high point of each day—not only was the food great, but even better were the attractive, young, Japanese women bringing it.

Approximately three weeks into the dismantling operations, the officers in charge decided to start giving all the soldiers and sailors one day off each week. As I remember it, we were given a briefing on how to stay safe if we left the Japanese naval facility. We were told to travel only in groups and that any kind of lewd or immoral conduct in any public place would not be tolerated. Engaging with prostitutes was completely forbidden and would be dealt with harshly. We were told not to give anything to beggars and to stay away from any Japanese soliciting. Loitering or wandering on private property was prohibited. Finally, disturbing the peace in any way would not be accepted.

When fully briefed, our crew was given liberty and we headed into Sasebo. The Japanese civilians seemed somewhat afraid of us, and despite viewing them as the enemy for months, I couldn't help but sympathize with them. After all, we had just decimated two of their cities, but I had no idea how severely damaged Sasebo had been from the American bombing over the last few months. Harsh memories of Caen flashed through my mind, because nearly 50 percent of the buildings were down or severely damaged. Japanese men, women, and children were still working on cleaning up the rubble. In Caen, I remember it being the British and Americans that cleaned up with heavy equipment and large groups of soldiers—very impersonal. What a difference from there to here. Of course, this was the enemy while the French were allies. I couldn't help but feel sorry for these people, knowing they never had a choice in the Japanese government's decision to start this war. After spending the day sight-seeing what was left of the city of Sasebo, we headed back to the harbor and prepared to return to duty the next day.

During the next few weeks, the dismantling operation, or "the de-industrializing," as the navy officers called it, continued just as planned.

The Japanese officer who had given me his sword had long since been dismissed. I had never actually needed his assistance. I continued touring the countryside and nearby towns on my days off every week. On these tours, I certainly could see that most Japanese people were unfortunately homeless and facing starvation. Inflation was rampant and many Japanese people had to turn to the black market for the most basic needs. Japanese women turned to prostitution as a means of feeding their families—the alternative was starvation. Abuse of homemade alcohol by many of the Japanese became a huge problem. For the first time in my life, I learned about the abuse of drugs and how this was yet another daunting problem the Japanese were facing. It was a pretty desperate situation for the Japanese. I think the severity of their plight affected me the most when I saw families sharing food with each other and their children that they had scavenged out of our military garbage cans. This may create a false impression that these were a bunch of uneducated people who lacked any kind of civilized behavior. I found that to be far from the truth. The Japanese were really a well-educated, good, and kind people with high morals from a wonderful ancient culture who had been forced into this lifestyle. It was almost unfathomable that a few government leaders had reduced their people to this way of life.

Unfortunately, some of our sailors began self-destructive behavior, such as consuming Japanese homemade alcohol, gambling, partaking in prostitution, and even using the black market to illegally procure desired items. Many of these men got away with all sorts of wrongdoing, while others paid quite a price for their misconduct.

All of us learned the new term "occupied Japan," which meant that Americans, with some help from the British, now occupied all of Japan. It had been somewhere around five months since the two atomic bombs had been dropped. From where we were stationed in Sasebo, it was about a two-hour drive southeast to Nagasaki, the city where the second bomb was dropped. Now that we had become familiar with the Japanese people and had learned how to safely move around the country, three other Chief Petty Officers and I decided to make a trip to Nagasaki to see the damage from the second bomb.

On a warmer day, we arranged to get a Jeep to make the two-hour trip. Along the way, we saw some of the massive damage that our American bombers had inflicted before the end of the war. We saw destroyed buildings, devastated roads, and bomb craters everywhere. It was a fate I wouldn't have wished on even my worst enemy. What I didn't expect to see were several crashed American airplanes along the way. Apparently, those were planes lost to the Japanese Zeros.

As we were nearing Nagasaki, I started seeing burn marks on trees, on the sides of buildings, and on anything that faced the city. Leaves on the trees were curled, misshaped, and scorched dry from a sudden exposure to heat. As we got even closer, the burn marks we saw got bigger and deeper until we were looking at trees and telephone poles that had been on fire on one entire side. Next there were a few trees down. Quickly the scene changed from most trees having no leaves on them at all to the majority completely down. We saw collapsed buildings that had burned after they were blown down. As we were approaching Nagasaki, I could see it was surrounded by huge mountains. Those same mountains that had once surrounded a thriving city were now surrounding nothing but a smoldering and charred crater.

Finally, we arrived at the blast zone. When we stopped the Jeep and got out, I could see for miles across the nearly barren landscape. Nearly everything was down. As I stood there, I could see a few building corners still standing, but the vast majority of the ground was covered with a couple of feet of metal, charred wood, stone, and brick. Tree trunks that looked like huge, burnt, wooden matches jutted up defiantly through the debris. Their branches no longer existed. Concrete and stone that was directly exposed to the blast was tanned dark with burn marks. It was easy to see how everything had been hurled outward from the blast. Anything in the rubble that was flammable had completely burned and was gone. It was truly a testament to how violent and destructive the nature of humanity could be.

When we returned to the Jeep, we moved along makeshift roads that had been pushed into existence by bulldozers. What I was seeing was almost unbelievable in its scope. As I looked across the devastation, it was obvious to me that this had been a large, industrial city. At some point we were looking at the remains of a factory that was still, almost incomprehensibly, standing. It was amazing to me that all the structures around this factory had been destroyed, but not the factory itself. More amazing was that the factory's smokestacks were still standing! Also astonishing to me were that the trains— both the engines and the cars in the area of the factory—had been thrown around like matchbox cars.

I saw a few Japanese people rummaging and searching through the rubble. It was interesting that one Japanese man was collecting and stacking roof tile, as I couldn't imagine that he had a house to put them on.

After spending the best part of a day touring the bombsite, we started the two-hour trip back to Sasebo. Not much was said by any of us. I think seeing the destruction of Nagasaki shook all of us to our core, and talking just didn't seem appropriate at the time. As we continued along the road, I was thinking about my time on the *Endure*, and the guys were saying that America should drop atom bombs on the whole country. Well, after learning to appreciate the plight of the innocent Japanese civilians and how the atom bomb had devastated them, I realized that it would have been wiser to say, "I hope to God we never have a reason to drop another atom bomb." God, it was awful ... just awful.

A few weeks after our trip to Nagasaki, the work of dismantling the Japanese Imperial Navy's shipyard was ending. At this same time, which was sometime in the beginning of 1946, there were a lot of replacement troops arriving in the country, taking the place of long-serving soldiers and the sailors who would be up for discharges. I was one of those long-serving fellows that got great news! I was informed that I was to rejoin the *Endure* and prepare for discharge.

Oh my God, I couldn't believe it. I was going home! It had been more than three and a half years that I had been on active duty, and it was finally over for me. I was going home! I boarded the *Endure* in Sasebo and joined a few other crew members being discharged as well. We had about a one-day trip to Wakayama, Japan, where we would board another ship for home. After nearly four years at war, I could hardly remember what it was like to be a civilian.

[CHAPTER 9]

Going Home

THE *Endure* SAILED TO WAKAYAMA, Japan, where those of us who were being discharged were dropped off and the *Endure*'s new replacements were picked up. After saying our farewells to the fellows we had served with, we disembarked the *Endure* for the last time. Next we were directed to a troop transport ship, which would be heading for America's west coast the next day.

I headed down to the docks where the transport ship was moored. Then, just as I did when leaving Europe, I talked to one of the ship's crewmembers. I made a deal with this fellow regarding loading my second duffel bag of Japanese souvenirs with some of the ship's cargo for ten cartons of cigarettes. We agreed that he would get five cartons now and another five cartons when we got to California. The plan was for him to ensure that the bag would be unloaded as soon as we landed so I wouldn't miss my next means of transportation. With that arrangement made, I boarded the transport ship.

I was told that there were going to be about five thousand men on board the ship. Most of these fellows were army troops heading home, as new recruits were replacing them in key locations of occupied Japan. This troopship wasn't fit-up to handle this many men, so temporary berthing areas were created by hanging hammocks in every available space on the ship. Conditions for the men assigned to these areas were very crowded, to say the least. I remember seeing men directed to berthing areas created in public areas and any available space that could be found within the ship. Men had to constantly climb over things to get into and out of their hammocks. Hammocks were aligned in rows and hung three high, with the man on the top almost touching the pipes and wires immediately above him.

I was much luckier than most of the other fellows going home. Being navy when making the trip home, I was assigned to duty in the engine room. I was to assist the chief of this engine room with systems checking. This gave me something to do to pass the time rather than just lying around, bored to death. With this assignment, I was also given a normal bunk to sleep in and was more like a regular crewmember.

I was standing on the ship's deck as we were pulling out of Wakayama, already thinking about "home sweet home." No one could imagine how eager I was to see my dad, my brothers and my sister after all this time away. I was equally anxious to find out how my brother Henry was doing and what his wartime experiences in the navy had been. I wondered who would get home first—would it be me or my brother Henry? I was looking forward to all five of us being together at home again. I was definitely picturing a reunion with the most important people in my life, and that reunion would be happening in the not-too-distant future. Then it hit me like a ton of bricks as I was picturing it—a reunion with the most important people in my life would have to include Tillins! Yes, Tillins would probably be contacting me. I felt sure he would, because when I was leaving Le Harve, I wrote a note and tied it to his backpack, giving him my home address and telling him to look me up after the war. *Yes,* I thought to myself, *when I get home I'll see my good friend Tillins again.* I couldn't wait to find out how he had finished out his duty. Thinking about seeing Tillins was definitely satisfying and made me feel very content. As I stood on deck looking out into the vastness of the ocean, I was smiling from ear to ear as I imagined our reunion.

By then we were underway and at the beginning of a two-week trip home to the USA! I was on duty in the engine room sometime after we left Japan during our first few hours at sea, running a check on all the systems in the engine room as well as preparing my paperwork for documenting all the readings I would be recording on the voyage home. While doing this, I saw something very strange. An army soldier had entered the engine room and made his way to the workbench. I watched from a distance as he took a deck of playing cards and sandwiched them between two pieces of wood. Then he clamped the combination tightly in the vise on the workbench. After he located a rather fine metal file, he began running it across the side of the playing cards, making one end of the deck just a hair thinner in width than the other end. He was shaving the deck of cards. I'd heard of a shaved deck before, but I hadn't really known exactly what it meant. After I saw what he was doing, the understanding of what a shaved deck is suddenly became very clear to me. You see, when the dealer of a shaved deck reverses one card, that card is then a little wider on one end of the deck than all the others. This kind of a deck would give the dealer the ability to pick a reversed card out of the deck at any time he chose. He took the cards out of the vise, looked around, didn't see me, and quickly left the engine room. *Boy*, I thought, *this fellow is going to get himself killed cheating at cards!*

Now that we had left Japan and were underway, many of the army fellows were up on the main deck getting cool, fresh air to avoid getting seasick. When we were several hours into our trip, we started getting into some rougher seas, which progressively got a little worse on the second and third days into the trip home. The smarter army fellows stood out on deck day and night, looking into the wind to avoid an upset stomach. The guys without "sea legs," who were just lying around below deck, began feeling the effects of seasickness and had some serious nausea from the constantly rough seas.

In the beginning of those first few hours of rough seas, I remember some of those army fellows joking about how the ship was like riding a roller coaster, but that joking ended when we hit some really high seas. In the highest of the rough seas, the ship would crest huge swells in the ocean, then it would drop off the front of those huge waves, then the bow of the ship would disappear under water for a few seconds. In a moment, it would reappear, and thousands of gallons of water would run off the front deck as we climbed the next ocean swell. By the second day of this kind of rocking and rolling, those same soldiers were sick and spending lots of time running to the bathroom and vomiting their guts out. The latrines were always disgusting and dirty as men got sicker and couldn't make it to the commode. The third day of rough seas was by far the worst. The smell below deck became awful; floors were constantly being mopped as the soldiers were getting even more seasick. The whole atmosphere for the army was horrible. Thank God the seas calmed down the fourth day and sailing became smooth and tranquil again. I think every army guy was up on the main deck as the muggy and musty smell of sweat and vomit was being aired out of the lower decks. The berthing areas were thoroughly cleaned, mopped, and sprayed with something to kill the revolting odor.

Unfortunately, the soldiers on board had nowhere to go, nothing to do, and nowhere to do it if there were something to do! This ship had no store, no library, and nothing in the way of recreation areas for the men, so these fellows were confined to hanging out in the sleeping quarters or walking the decks. During rainy weather and at night, the men spent most of their time in their bunks lying around doing nothing. All day long, men just sat around telling war stories, reading outdated magazines, playing cards, or rolling dice in the poorly lit, overcrowded, makeshift berthing area.

At least we had good food to eat—three full meals a day and plenty of it. At midnight, a fourth meal was served, which was a combination of all the leftovers from that day. Compared to the normal foods I had eaten for the last three and a half years, these seemed like meals fit for a king!

About halfway through the voyage home on an evening while I was off duty, I was walking around the ship just killing time. I heard some friendly commotion; a lot of laughing and hooting was coming from one of the temporary berthing areas. I went in to see what was amusing the fellows. When I got inside, the first thing I saw was a large group of soldiers standing and watching another group of soldiers sitting on buckets, playing cards around a large wooden crate. To my amazement, the card dealer was the same fellow I had seen shaving the deck of cards in the engine room! I stood back and watched as he coaxed soldiers to bet on card cutting.

He would thoroughly shuffle the cards, and then he would hand the deck to another player to cut the cards. After the second player cut the cards, he would flip the top card over and say, "Okay, over or under." The fellows around the table would lay down dollar bills in different piles, betting on whether or not cutting the rest of the deck in half would reveal a card higher or lower than the card flipped. When a 2, 3, or 4 came up, no one would bet. Likewise, when a queen, king, or ace came up there were no takers. When a 7, 8, or 9 was flipped, the dollars went down on piles as these fellows gambled on the next card being higher or lower. Betting on the middle cards was more or less a fifty-fifty chance of winning or losing a dollar. The risky bet was betting lower on a 5 or 6, or betting higher on a 10 or a Jack.

As I watched this guy deal the cards, I knew he was a cheat, but now I also saw that he was a shrewd showman. He was constantly talking and laughing as he challenged the other fellows to bet. Then he began prompting and challenging fellows to side bet or bet against each other outside the main pot. After a while, it was like five or six separate games were being played at once. As the dealer, he would confirm each group was done betting before he cut the deck that revealed the winning or losing card.

Now here's the scam. When one of the side games had a large pot going on and everybody was focusing on that game, our swindler would look at the deck's bottom card. He would then, with one hand, turn that card 180 degrees. When he shuffled the deck for the next hand, he could pick this one turned card out of the shaved deck at any time. This gave him the ability to make a winning bet every time. He was smart; he lost a few and he won a few. In fact, he lost most every small pot, saying loudly, "Lost again." When the pots he was in got larger, he would bet a little more and win a little more. He was a real con man, slowly winning more and more money, never really letting the rest of the group notice how his overall winnings kept growing, as he always was focusing on someone else's winning of larger pots.

If I had exposed this guy, I don't think he would have made it home alive. There would have been a good chance somebody, or even a group of fellows who lost a lot of money, would do something pretty unscrupulous to get even. Many of those fellows saw lots of death and dying in Okinawa and wouldn't think twice about slaying one more individual. Nope, I wasn't going to be responsible for this man's death. It was time for me to get ready to go back on duty, so I left the card game and headed back to my quarters.

The next day when I was getting something to eat in the ship's galley, I heard a couple of fellows talking about what a great time they were having gambling. They went on and on about this hand and that fellow and how today they were going to play the odds differently. As they talked, I could tell none of them was ahead, but it didn't seem to bother them. They were headed home, the war was over, and life was good. I heard them say they had just received their sixty dollars of monthly pay and planned to have fun whether they lost it all or not. One of them said that when he got home he would worry about all the business of establishing a responsible lifestyle. Until then, he planned to celebrate living through the war, have fun, and spend lots of time laughing. Hearing that made me realize that losing a month's pay of sixty dollars was far from the worst thing that could happen in this world. In the big picture, it really didn't mean anything.

After eating, I made my way to the berthing area where the gambling was going on. Again, there sat the con man dealing cards and working the crowd. I watched for a while and then finally placed a side bet based on what I saw happening in the dealer hand. I won and placed another bet, winning again. Watching the dealer and what he was doing gave me an advantage even he didn't have. I was careful not to win too much, and I built my winnings slowly. By the end of that session, I was ahead about two hundred dollars. In 1945 that was equal to a little more than a month of the average civilian's pay. I didn't flash my money; I didn't tell the other players how much I had won. I kept changing my betting from side bet to side bet. The other fellows playing did know I was ahead, but I didn't let them know *how much* I was ahead. I started gambling between nearly every shift, slowly and cautiously building my winnings. By the time the cruise home was almost over, I was a couple of thousand dollars ahead and never heard one other man grumble, gripe, or complain about my winnings.

After about two full weeks at sea, we were sailing into the San Diego, California, naval base. As we pulled into port, bands were playing, flags were flying, and there were rejoicing crowds of civilians there to welcome us home. The captain of our ship was blowing the ship's horn with long, loud blasts. Many of the soldiers and sailors from towns and cities near the West Coast had family there to greet their returning loved ones. Lots of tears of joy were being shed by both people in the crowd and many of the soldiers on board as we came into the dock. It was all somewhat overwhelming and very gratifying to see crowds of civilians there cheering for their returning soldiers. Everyone returning home was treated as if he were a war hero. I will never forget that feeling.

We were told to let the West Coast fellows get off the ship first so they could greet their families as quickly as possible. With that in mind, I was standing and waiting at the rail on the main deck, watching fellows unload and meet their families. All of a sudden, the fellow next to me said, "Hey, I know you. You're that guy who was riding my coattails while gambling." I looked over to see that it was the card shark who had shaved the deck. Before I could say a word, he said, "You made a lot of money following my lead. You're the only one who figured out the game. Good for you. At least you were smart enough to keep quiet and just play along. You know, you'll have a good start on life when you get home. You can thank me for that." Before I could say a word, he turned and started walking away, then stopped for a second, turned around, and said, "Good luck, kid." What could I say?

I continued standing at the rail, watching family reunion after family reunion. The reason I was taking so much time was that I needed to hang around until I could pick up my duffel bag of Japanese souvenirs. With that in mind, I was one of the last fellows off the ship. The timing worked out just fine. Within minutes of getting off the ship, I had exchanged five more cartons of cigarettes for my souvenirs, and shortly after that was boarding a large, green army bus on the next leg of my trip home.

The bus ride was short, only taking a few minutes and ending up in a railroad yard only a few miles inland. There we were loaded into boxcars that would be heading east. I remember climbing into an old railroad car and taking my place sitting on the floor with a few dozen other fellows. Within a few minutes, I heard the locomotive's whistle sound off. Next, the car hitches clanged as the railroad cars' couplings were pulled forward, and wheels squealed as they began to turn. Then I heard the sound of the wind as we started to sway from side to side in the heat of a southwestern United States desert. The floor of the boxcar was dusty and gritty, and the wooden floorboards and walls smelled moldy and musty. We traveled with the doors on either side of the car about halfway open to allow in light and fresh air. As we moved through the desert, I could smell the coal smoke from the steam engine that was pulling the long row of boxcars.

As I lay back against the wall, I thought back to how I had spent the last few years. Tillins was the first thought that ran through my mind as I pictured him saying, "You know, Bill, a fellow could get killed around here." Just thinking about Tillins made me smile and shake my head. We had started this journey through hell together, and now that it was coming to an end, I wished he was there so we could see it through all the way to the end together. I sure hoped it wouldn't be long until I heard from him. Then there were memories of Corky and what a nice fellow he was. I had recollections of the thirty minutes we spent trying to get off Omaha Beach, which at the time felt like an eternity. I recalled fighting street-to-street in Caen, our friend Frenchy, driving supplies to the Battle of the Bulge, towing duties in the South Pacific, and sweeping mines off the coast of Japan. All of these memories flashed vividly through my mind as I relived all the amazement, fear, and hardships of the past three and a half years. I thought to myself, *It was one hell of a run, one maybe even worth putting down on paper. You know, I should really think about writing a book.*

[CHAPTER 10]

After the War

AFTER THE WAR, I WAITED to hear from Tillins. For some reason, he hadn't contacted me. I started to wonder if he hadn't made it. The end of 1946 came, then 1947, then 1948. By 1949, I was sure my good buddy was killed during the war. Then the strangest thing happened in the summer of 1950. I was driving through Philadelphia in a rainstorm in a high-rise part of the city when I stopped at a traffic light that had three separate lanes. I was sitting in the left-turn-only lane. To my immediate right was the straight-through lane, and to my far right was a right-turn-only lane. That's when I heard *beep-beep, beep-beep, beep-beep* from a car in the far right lane. I looked over and saw Tillins hitting his horn, waving his hand, and hollering from an open window in the pouring rain. "Hey Bill, Bill, Bill! Hey, hey, Bill, Bill!"

"Tillins, Tillins you son-of-a-bitch, Tillins!" I stepped out of my pickup truck and hollered over to Tillins. "Hey Tillins! Listen, Tillins, pull around the corner and wait for me. I'll go around the block and meet you there in a minute."

"Okay, Bill."

As soon as the light changed, I rushed around the block. When I got back to the intersection, I pulled over, parked my truck, and jumped out in a hurry. I looked right and left to spot Tillins. As I was looking, I kept thinking, *Okay Tillins, where did you park?* I ran up to the intersection, looking around. No Tillins there. I ran down the street about half way, crossed over, and then ran back up to the intersection, checking both sides. Still no Tillins. *Damn, he must be further down the street.* On my second pass, I ran all the way to the intersection at the other end of the street, crossed over, and ran half way back the other side. Still no Tillins. *He must be on one of the other three streets adjacent to the intersection where we met*, I thought. It was still raining hard as I ran to each street, looking to see if I could spot Tillins. Finally, I just stood in the rain on the corner at the intersection where we had first seen each other. *He must be driving around in his car*, I thought. *I'll just wait here until he sees me.*

For about thirty minutes I stood on that corner in the rain, just looking around and hoping Tillins would show up. He never showed. I couldn't imagine what happened. I don't know why he didn't wait for me. Why did he even blow the horn? I slowly walked back to my truck, got in, and headed home. At least I knew he was alive.

"Just recently I tried to locate Tillins again. With my daughter's help, we searched the Internet using several different websites dedicated to finding people. We spent several weeks searching and checking, but we never found Tillins. The closest match was a man with the same name who had died of cancer in the early 1990s. Who knows, maybe that was him. The whole Philadelphia encounter still upsets me today."

-Bill Grannetino, 1998

[THE AFTERWORD]

AFTER THE WAR, BILL GRANNETINO started his working career employed in the construction industry. Within a few short years of working for other people, Bill started his own construction company. After several years of successfully working as a contractor, he shifted his line of business to the trucking industry. The incentive to switch career fields came when Bill was building a maintenance terminal for a large trucking organization and then, at their request, accepted a position as their superintendent in charge of maintaining a large fleet of tractor and trailer trucks. After a few years of employment with this large firm, Bill moved on and started his own trucking company, transporting steel and petroleum products. While operating this trucking company, Bill was extremely successful, which produced a prosperity he had not anticipated.

With this additional unanticipated surplus in capital, Bill started investing his money in a variety of ways. These investments quickly grew, creating an even greater abundance of resources for further investing opportunities. Once reinforced with now-substantial funds, he looked for greater opportunities in stocks and other investing prospects. Against the recommendations of his bankers and brokers, he speculated on some extremely risky financial investments. Those investments eventually paid off so well that Bill sold his trucking business and retired at the age of fifty-five with ample financial security to live out the remainder of his life.

Another notable fact about Bill's career was that he occasionally offered his mechanical abilities and career experience as a consultant in several different mechanical and industrial fields. He consulted on such things as the design of drain oil burning furnaces, industrial engines, and turbines for the movement of bulk materials like Portland cement. He was retained as a consultant to assist with the set-up of a turbine for a winning Indianapolis 500 race car. He set-up a cement plant in South America and solved bulk material handling problems in a factory in California. On another occasion, he enhanced production in a sand quarry, doubling production with fewer people. These were just a few of his many endeavors and achievements.

Bill was married in 1948 and was a devoted husband and father of eight children. Widowed after thirty-eight years, Bill later enjoyed the company of a second partner for the remaining years of his life. About the time Bill's second partner passed away, Bill was moved to a nursing home while in the advanced stages of Alzheimer's. He lived out the final two years of his life in the nursing home before dying at the age of eighty-seven in 2011. Regardless of his suffering from the advanced effects of Alzheimer's, the one thing he never forgot was the day he landed on Omaha Beach.

CPSIA information can be obtained
at www.ICGtesting.com
Printed in the USA
LVHW090442080222
710542LV00017B/458/J